TROJAN
HORSES

A STORY OF HOMEGROWN TERRORISM

Sheldon Cohen

authorHOUSE®

AuthorHouse™
1663 Liberty Drive
Bloomington, IN 47403
www.authorhouse.com
Phone: 1 (800) 839-8640

Published by AuthorHouse 05/21/2018

ISBN: 978-1-5049-1312-6 (sc)
ISBN: 978-1-5049-1313-3 (e)

Print information available on the last page.

Any people depicted in stock imagery provided by Thinkstock are models,
and such images are being used for illustrative purposes only.
Certain stock imagery © Thinkstock.

This book is printed on acid-free paper.

Because of the dynamic nature of the Internet, any web addresses or links contained in
this book may have changed since publication and may no longer be valid. The views
expressed in this work are solely those of the author and do not necessarily reflect the
views of the publisher, and the publisher hereby disclaims any responsibility for them.

DEDICATION

**I dedicate this book to
Betty,
Gail, Paul, Marci,
Amanda, Shane, Megan, Travis,
Carly, Alexa, Ethan, Emily,
Derek, Rylie, Benjamin.**

ALSO BY SHELDON COHEN

CHAPTER 1

MADISON, WISCONSIN

Ben Marzan:

As Ben Marzan, deep in thought, walked down his high school corridor, he bumped into a fellow student. His large brown eyes stared for one second, and without a word or change of expression, rage replaced the differential equations of his thoughts. At five feet nine inches and weighing 172 pounds, he lashed out and struck the student's right cheek with a powerful closed open hand. His much taller and heavier opponent reeled back for a second, regained his composure, and with eyes burning fire grabbed Ben's ponytail, threw him to the floor and landed on top of him with two clenched fists being brought into position ready to strike. However, before he could wreak his intended havoc, Ben wrapped both of his legs around his opponent's waist and thrust him to the side with a leg strength that brought a look of amazement to the group of students that had quickly assembled. He then grabbed his opponent's right arm and twisted it until he cried for mercy. It took three other male students pulling them apart to save the hapless victim from at least a possible dislocated shoulder. Two teachers, attracted by the noise, grabbed Ben by both arms and accompanied him to the principal's office. He went without resistance—a defiant expression on his face.

When the principal saw him, he sighed, shrugged his shoulders and said, "It's you, Ben? What a surprise. Have a seat." Both teachers explained to the principal what they had witnessed. Ben sat, head down staring at his palms.

The principal watched Ben for a moment, then turned to his surly visitor and said, "Do you want to tell me what happened, Ben?"

Ben's bulging eyes stared at the principal for five seconds before he answered in a slow and deliberate monotone, "He bumped into me. I responded. Simple as that."

"He bumped into you or you bumped into him? Could you tell? Could it have been an accident on his part if he did the bumping?" If you did the bumping, why would you lash out at him? This type of behavior has to stop before you do something that will ruin your life. You've got to learn to take a second to think before you act."

There was no answer from Ben. The principal interpreted a bored look on Ben's face. "It's okay for you to go, gentlemen, I want to speak with our friend alone."

"There's nothing to talk about," said Ben without making eye contact.

"There is if I say there is," said the principal in a firm voice. "We've got a lot to talk about." Ben turned his gaze toward the principle. His face was a stony mask.

"I know all about you, Ben. You're a fine student according to your record. You get nothing but A's on your tests, but how do you expect that to reflect on your grades when you never hand in homework or do assignments. We have strict rules here at Madison West. Homework assignments go toward your final grade just like quizzes and tests. You're lucky your teachers are lenient with you. They'd have every justification to flunk you. Your attendance is about as bad as any student we've ever had. Why is that?"

Without a change of expression and with a low monotone, Ben said, "It's a waste of time."

"Why did I figure you'd say something like that? Even though you're bored, at least make a pretence of listening. You'll always find yourself in difficulty at work or at school if you show your boredom like that. That kind of attitude sends a message of disrespect, and that will hinder your progress. Don't squander what could be great potential. I have seen three students in the last twenty-five years get a perfect SAT score and you're one of them. You've got to learn to control your emotions before it's too late."

"I have to go now," said Ben opening and closing both hands and moving his upper body in a coordinated rhythmic manner. The sudden disruption in his daily after-school ritual put him in an agitated state that the principal recognized in spite of Ben's mask-like facial expression.

"Calm down. It's over. Why are you so agitated?"

"I'm late. I got someplace to go."

"Where are you going in such a hurry, may I ask?"

"To the gym."

Recognizing the calm before a potential storm, the principal said, "Okay, you're free to go, but we're not finished with this yet. I'll be calling your parents. If there is any repetition of this kind of behavior, you're in serious trouble. Do you understand?"

There was no response from Ben as he turned around and walked out of the office leaving the principal staring at his back.

Head down, deeply in thought, Ben Marzan walked to his high school locker to pick up his gym bag. He would spend an hour after school working with weights at the nearby health club, something he had been doing ever since his freshman year almost four years ago. It had become a ritual, and missing this hour would only happen, as he liked to say, 'in a dire emergency.'

The health club was a ten-minute walk from Madison West High School in Madison, Wisconsin, and he viewed the walk as a warm-up enabling him to get immediately to the heavy weights. When he arrived, he promptly went into his weight-lifting regimen. The last ten minutes of this exercise time was spent winding down with a half mile speed run.

Even when Ben was lifting weights, math far beyond the high school level was on his mind, and there was no one in school that he could confer with so he conferred with himself. The majority of time his thoughts were on the latest math problem that he was attempting to solve. It was as if his brain was equipped with a piece of chalk that could write the complex mathematical symbols on a blackboard in easy view of his mind that could view and erase and change numbers and symbols as necessary.

During math tests, Ben did so little written work on the test paper that his teachers would accuse him of cheating. They didn't believe that he could do all the mathematical steps in his mind and come up with the correct answer until he demonstrated his ability by having them give him a problem that he would work in the teacher's presence. He would stare at the problem for a moment, chalk in a few barely discernable notes, stare some more, write an equal sign and then the answer. All his mathematics teachers throughout his four years came to grips with this exceptional talent and let him do his own thing. They even accepted the fact that he rarely handed in homework. He had proven that whatever he was doing to learn math, it was more than enough. His teachers knew that mathematics like any other of life's endeavors took practice. It was one thing to learn a technique, but another to understand and be able to work the problems each of which had different twists—and that is why it was necessary to practice in order to learn the various paths to a solution. One of his teachers likened Ben to Ramanujan, an Indian mathematician who made significant contributions to number theory, continued fractions and mathematical analysis in the late nineteenth and early twentieth century, and was too intimidated to accept Ben as a pupil, suggesting he teach himself rather than, "Waste my time. He should be the one teaching me."

CHAPTER 2

Hari and Lois Marzan:

Ben's relationship with his parents was similar to his relationship with his fellow students in the sense that his parents could not easily predict his mood. They were never quite sure how to act in his presence. Nor could they predict what word or action of theirs might trigger an unfavorable response. This caused tension between his mother and father as they often could not agree on what approach to take with their unpredictable son.

The father, Hari, came to the United States from Pakistan when he was a young man. He was a precocious youngster who came from one of the tribal areas of Waziristan who worked on his father's farm. This would remain his fate had it not been for the intervention of one of the local Imams who, while studying the Koran with the youngster, recognized his mathematical potential at an early age.

The Imam appealed to Hari's father and urged him to let Hari go to school in Peshawar where he could tap into what the Imam felt was a mathematical potential that must not dissipate on the farm. "Your son could bring back the days of the great, glorious Islamic mathematicians," he said. The Imam's reputation was such that the father agreed, so Hari took a placement test and received a full scholarship to the University of Peshawar.

After completing undergraduate studies, he obtained a Ph.D. in mathematics at Northwestern University in Evanston, Illinois and settled down to a career as a teacher and researcher in the mathematics department of the University of Wisconsin. He married a wealthy American-born heiress from Madison. Hari was a devout Muslim, and his wife, Lois, converted to Islam. They gave their son a solid Islamic upbringing, but this did not change the rebellion that they and Ben's teachers knew only too well.

The principal of Ben's school called Lois the next morning. He wasted no time in getting into the details of Ben's recent altercation. "Your son was fighting in the hallways, Ms. Marzan. Two teachers brought him to my office. We had a talk, and I have to tell you he was a bit rude. I'm concerned about his attitude. He's an incredible intellect, but I'm afraid he's going to squander his potential."

Lois slumped in her chair. Others had told her the same thing. "I'm sorry, sir, I'll have a talk with him. Was he hurt in any way?"

"No, he wasn't. From what I understand, it was the other boy that got the worst of it, but no major damage, Ms. Marzan, nothing to worry about."

Lois breathed a sigh of relief. "Thank God for that," she said.

"This is not the first time this has happened, Ms. Marzan. There is a pattern here, I believe. His attitude is—what shall I say—different from his peers. It makes me wonder if a consultation with a mental health professional would be in order? It's your choice, of course, but if you'd like a quick evaluation, we could offer the school psychologist, Dr. Levine."

This was something Lois did not want to hear, but at the same time, she was not surprised. This nagging thought had been on her mind and was already a source of conflict with her husband. She sighed and closed her eyes. "I'll talk this over with my husband when he comes home tonight, and I'll get back to you tomorrow," she replied.

As she sat back in her favorite recliner, she revisited the fear that there might indeed be something wrong with their son, Ben. She worried that his intense interest in mathematics disrupted his concentration. He was an only child. She herself was an only child. She had always led a sheltered existence, growing up in the house of a prominent Wisconsin surgeon and his socialite wife.

She was five feet four inches, and was very attractive with dark brown hair and hazel eyes now shimmering with tears. Yes, we've got to do something, she thought, I'll have it out with Hari when he gets home.

When her husband arrived, she let him settle in before she spoke with him. He had a specific ritual that she knew better not to disturb. He would have to get out of his suit, put on some leisure clothes and slippers, spend a few minutes scanning the paper before it was wise to speak with him. "I have news about your son, Hari."

"My son? When it's my son, that means I'm not going to get pleasant news. What happened now?"

She spared no detail telling him about the fight at school and the principle's phone call and his recommendations.

"What is he suggesting," said Hari. "Does he think that Ben should see a psychiatrist?" He got off his recliner and walked over to the table where Lois was sitting. He sat down across the table from her. This told her that it was a good time to get deeper into the discussion. His wife stared into his penetrating dark eyes. His full head of black hair, combed without a hair out of place when he would leave for work every morning, was ruffled. This contrasted with his perfectly groomed salt and pepper beard. He was a serious man, very analytic in his thinking, inbred from years of concentration on advanced mathematical thinking—and his facial expression reflected this mindset.

Lois quickly took advantage of his body language message and said, "He used the words mental health professional, and he said if we were interested he would let him see the school psychologist, Dr. Levine. It looks to me like that's the quickest way to get an opinion. We shouldn't pass this up."

"Yes, you're right. We have to help Ben, but the method—that's what we have to think about."

A puzzled Lois asked, "What do you mean the method? What is there to think about?"

"There's more than one way to get help. I don't have much faith in the American mental health system of care. I have friends who go to get help. They get put in a clinic setting and never even see a doctor. This counselor, that counselor; it's all secular. It has nothing to do with religion. God has no place in it. Ben needs more than what they have to offer in this country."

Lois leaned forward with her forehead creased, tears in her eyes and lips closed. Then she blurted out, "More than one way? What more ways are there? We have to leave it to the professionals, people trained in such disciplines."

Hari answered reassuringly. "Calm, be calm. You're right. We do have to leave it to the professionals, but it's a matter of defining the word professional. You feel it's a medical professional. I have a different viewpoint. I agree that you and I have had no luck with our son. Yes, he needs help. We will give him that help. I know what he needs. He needs to come closer to Allah. That's what he needs. He needs God in his life." Then after a long pause, Hari slowly and seriously said, "That he cannot get from doctors, nurses, or counselors."

She slumped back in her chair. "You've tried that more than once and nothing happened? What would it hurt to let him see the school psychologist at least one time?"

"Is once enough?" "I don't think so. What does the psychologist know? I've been trying for years to get the boy on the right path. We're both too emotionally involved. You think a psychologist will see him once, and he will come to Allah and all his quirks will be gone. You're dreaming, my dear wife."

"All I know is that he graduates in three months and starts college soon. He still doesn't know what he wants to do with his life. If he acts the same way in college as he's acting in high school, what'll happen? I worry about his future. I think we need to do something soon," Lois said with tears rolling down her cheeks.

Hari shook his head as he stared at his wife who he recognized was reaching a point of desperation. Then with finality he said, "Okay, okay. I'll go along with you for a while. I'll give one month to see what happens. It will take time for me to arrange spiritual help. You call the principal tomorrow and tell him that it is okay for him to see the school psychologist, three or four times if necessary. The psychologist should talk to his teachers before she sees Ben and get feedback from them. Then we'll talk to her and see what she thinks. We will see what happens with a neutral third party. You and I are having no success."

Lois wiped her tears and nodded yes.

CHAPTER 3

Psychological evaluation:

At the insistence of his parents, but with reluctance, Ben went to see Dr. Levine. When she found out that he was coming—and with the suggestion from Hari in mind—she spoke with two of his teachers to get their opinions. They both were as one in their beliefs. They gave Dr. Levine the impression that unless Ben's mental state could be turned around, his great intellectual potential would be wasted, because there was no telling what he could accomplish—especially in the mathematical and/or scientific arena where he knew more than any of his teachers. This was the consensus of the two that Dr. Levine spoke with, so out of curiosity she spoke with two more and it was unanimous.

Dr. Levine was fifty years of age, married with two children. She was full-figured and wore no make-up. There was no shortage of consultative evaluations in this large upper middle class predominantly white teen-age population and this kept her very busy.

Ben showed up on time and sat on the edge of the chair in front of the psychologist's desk. He glanced at a Ph.D. certificate hanging on the wall, and a picture of Ms. Levine and her husband and two teen-age children on the corner of her desk. Then he stared at Dr. Levine, noting her staring back at him over her reading glasses. He folded his arms across his chest. She smiled. "I'm glad you could make it. Can you tell me please, what happened between you and your classmate?"

He answered with a stern, unchanged expression on his face, "It's of no consequence. He's an ignorant, illiterate asshole." He uncrossed his arms, sat back in the chair for an instant, then leaned forward, put both elbows on the arms of the chair, put his hands in a prayer position in front of his face and stared at the psychologist over his fingertips.

"I need to understand why you reacted like you did, Ben. How can I understand if you won't tell me anything?"

With that, he leaped to his feet and walked back and forth in front of his interviewer. "There's nothing to understand. He's the one you should be interviewing, not me. I don't want to waste a single cubic centimeter of oxygen on that cretin."

Spoken like one with a mathematical and scientific background, she thought. As he continued talking, Dr. Levine said, "Why are you so agitated?"

"Agitated is right. Can I get the hell out of here?"

"Please sit down."

"I like standing."

"Don't you want to talk anymore?"

"You got that right, Ma'm, I don't."

She remained calm in the face of Ben's verbal onslaught. What little she knew from this few minutes of talking to her new client told her there may well be a problem. She decided not to push this interview further. She calmly said, "You have to be here Friday, you know. Your parents are expecting me to see you more than once," she said to his back as he nodded his head, turned and left the room.

He did return on Friday, ordered by his father after he received a call from the psychologist. Dr. Levine was shocked at the difference in her patient. She tried not to let her facial expression betray her thoughts. He walked in, hands in his pockets, eyes half closed and head nodded forward. He seemed to be in a dream state, or was his mind just occupied with other thoughts. He took a seat, both arms in his lap, palms down. He stared past his interviewer.

"How are you today?" she asked.

"Okay," he said with no visible lip movement.

"Do you feel all right?"

"Yeah."

"Have you seen that boy you had the fight with?"

"Yeah."

"Did anything happen?"

"No."

Through this brief discussion, his expressionless face remained unchanged. On one occasion, he turned his right hand palm up, flexed his fingers, and stared at his fingernails.

"Do you want to tell me anything at all?"

"Nothing to tell," he said in a monotone.

"Nothing? Did you have any problem with your fellow students this week?"

"No."

"Are your parents okay?"

"Yes they are fine."

"Would you tell me something about them."

"Nothing to tell."

"What do you plan to do with your life after you graduate, Ben?"

"College."

"Where?"

"Northwestern University in Evanston, Illinois."

"Are you looking forward to it?"

Ben grunted.

"What will you study?"

"Don't know."

And so the questions went for another fifteen minutes. He sat the entire time, changing his body position often. Dr. Levine met with him twice more in the next week. Both times, he exhibited a short attention span, answering all questions with as few words as possible and at times interspersed with four-letter words. Complicated as this case was, Ms. Levine felt that she could now offer some suggestions, so she arranged an appointment with his parents.

CHAPTER 4

Psychological impression:

They arrived in her office after school. The introductions complete, Dr. Levine couldn't help but notice the resemblance between Ben and his father—the same unsmiling, serious face. "Thank you for coming, Dr. and Ms. Marzan. I've seen your boy and I have some thoughts for you."

"And what do you think, doctor," said Hari.

"The times I saw him it was like talking to two different people. He vacillated between slight agitation and perhaps some depression. If I have to think of a psychiatric illness, I would tentatively suspect that he has either a bipolar disorder also known as manic depression, or he has an agitated depression. His teachers seem to think that math is engrossing him more than it should."

"It sounds confusing, Dr. Levine," said an alarmed Lois.

"Yes, I agree. Adolescents who develop one of these illnesses show the same depression and withdrawal and sometimes hopelessness as adults do, but they also can show extreme agitation and irritability, or they can demonstrate severe rage, use profanity, and have long lasting tantrums. The good news is that many of these people are highly intelligent, and if they can learn to stabilize their emotions, they can become very valuable citizens. One thing I spotted in your son is that he is a very intelligent youngster, even a genius perhaps. His teachers all said the same thing and had no doubt about his intellectual potential."

"What should we do?" asked Lois.

"I would first recommend a psychiatrist to confirm or deny one of these diagnoses. Then treatment can start if he or she concurs. It may well be that medication would be helpful. As a psychologist, I can't prescribe them in this state."

Hari, who had been slumping in the chair, leaned forwarded stiff-backed and said, "Treatment with medicine?"

The way that he responded told Ms. Levine that the thought of medicine was anathema to Hari, but she dealt with the problem directly, and in an authoritative a voice as possible, she exclaimed, "Yes. The two mainstays of therapy are medication and psychotherapy. Medicine can deal with the medical aspects of the illness, and psychotherapy, or talk therapy, helps the patients to understand their illness and develop the proper approaches to lessen the effects and reduce the hills and valleys."

"You say talk therapy?" asked Hari with wide opened eyes and a creased forehead.

"Yes, very important."

"May I ask a question, Ms. Levine?" asked Hari.

"Of course."

"What do you feel about just the use of talk therapy without medicine?"

"I understand your concern, Dr. Marzan. There is no such thing as a risk-free medicine. One or both, talk and medication, can be used together or alone as therapy. Actually, the choice of therapy always rests with the patient.

"Thank you, Dr. Levine. We appreciate the time you spent with our son." Hari delivered this last remark with a finality that told Dr. Levine, and his wife, the interview was over.

"You're welcome. If there's anything more I can do, please do not hesitate to ask", said Dr. Levine politely.

CHAPTER 5

Decision:

Hari and Lois drove home in silence. Lois noted her husband's expression and knew he was deep in thought. This meant she would hear his opinion soon—and she was right. They sat down at the kitchen table. "I know what we must do," said Hari.

With an anxiety based upon many years of experience learning to read her husband's tone of voice, all she could muster was a concerned "What?"

"I was thinking of this even before Ben saw Dr. Levine. I agree with you. It wouldn't be wise to send Ben to college now. He's too young. He's never adjusted well in school. He stays bored because everything is so easy for him. He has not found his true destiny because he does not know Allah. It all must be changed," Hari said very slowly.

Lois looked at her husband with trepidation. "How?" she murmured in fear assuming that this was a lead-in to his Allah based cure.

"He will go to the Imam for a year. He is not ready for college. He must learn that there is peace and contentment in knowing Allah. We will save our son," Hari said slowly and emphatically.

Lois sat up stiff-backed, her clasped hands in front of her mouth. "Oh my God; the Imam. You're talking Pakistan. You can't mean it." The last four words were delivered in a pleading voice, but Lois knew her husband's voice was spoken with the inflection that suggested an order—not anything to discuss.

"I mean it. You heard Dr. Levine. Talk therapy is what he needs. Twenty-five years ago in Pakistan, the Imam turned my life around. We were both young then. I was floundering like Ben. The Imam took me in tow and led me into math. I never knew I had an aptitude. Even though he was not much older than I was, he had the reputation of a Koran genius far beyond his young years. When the old Imam died, he stepped in and filled his shoes. His knowledge is beyond that of psychiatrists. God whispers in his ear. Where could Ben get better talk therapy than from the Imam? It is settled. I'll talk to Ben."

Lois responded, "What about medicine that Dr. Levine recommended?"

"The Imam will know. Medicines can be dangerous. What is wrong with a trial of talk therapy first? I believe that would make the use of medicines unnecessary. What are medicines? They are all poisons. Taken in a small dose they might help a person, but you never know. In big, enough doses—they kill, or they maim. Believe me I have studied the issue. Some of the psychiatric medicines leave permanent physical effects. Some of them lead to suicide. Medicine to me is a last resort."

"But you are acting as his doctor now. You are making the decision as to what he will or will not do. How could you do this? The medical professionals have a tough enough time trying to make therapy decisions, and you are trying to do that, and for your own son! That is reckless. What if, God forbid, something should happen to Ben. How would you feel? Don't do this, Hari."

Lois had never seen her husband get angry. He had a flat affect, but as his wife spoke in opposition to his thinking, his voice became louder—calm, but louder. Lois knew that this was his way of letting her know that his position was final and he would brook no opposition. What could she do? She feared for her son.

"My dear wife, Allah is the only tried and true medicine. Ben needs Allah. He will find him with the Imam."

"But you haven't spoken to the Imam for many years. How do you know what he thinks now? What if he's changed?"

"Changed? What do you mean? The Koran does not change. The Koran is the word of God. Allah does not rewrite his commandments. They're good for the duration of the universe."

"But there are those who interpret the Koran in different ways. They believe in the theory that the end justifies the means, and you know what kind of thinking that can lead to."

He spoke again as if he did not even hear her pleading and picked up his point from where he left off. "Think my dear wife. How would the world be if everybody in it adopted the Koran? If all rules were followed and penalties were so harsh that the rules would dare not be broken? There would be no sexually transmitted diseases. There would be no wars. There would be no crime. There would be no mental illness. We would have paradise on earth. That is the purpose of any religion."

Not yet allayed of her fears, Lois said again, this time with emphasis, "But I'm talking about the kind of thinking that leads to violence and terrorism. How do you know if the Imam hasn't changed? What if he has adopted a violent approach like some clerics we have heard. What kind of a man is he now? We have to know."

Surprised at this unusual show of emotion from his wife, Hari continued in a calm, instructing voice, "I know! What kind of a man? I will tell you. Your son needs simple and profound messages that will change the way he thinks. The Imam will give him this just as he gave it to me. What kind of a man was Mohammad? What kind of a man was Churchill in 1940? What kind of a man was Roosevelt in 1933? What kind of a man was Jesus and Moses and Mohammad. These are men that gave great messages, and they offered answers to the questions that their people wanted to have answered. Churchill warned his people to expect "blood, toil, tears and sweat," and overnight his citizens accepted that. Roosevelt told his people that, "the only thing we have to fear is fear itself," and it gave the people strength. Even a man like Lenin offered the Russians peace, land and bread, and they followed him with that hope. These are simple messages. These are eloquent messages. These messages are straightforward, forceful messages. These are messages that can turn lives around and change a world. The Imam has these messages, and he has the stature to have his words accepted and may alter the way a person thinks. Who needed such messages more than I did? Who needs those messages more than my son? Who needs these messages more than this world?"

Hari stopped speaking. His eyes shone, and his face looked toward the heavens. This was enough to tell his wife that interrupting him would be reckless for he had passed into an almost trance-like state and a disruption at this time would disturb his train of thought. That happened only once before, and she would never forget the change in her husband; the anger that was like a raging bull. She waited.

Still looking upward, he continued, "The Imam is intelligent but doesn't flaunt it. He is humble, and you sense it. He has climbed the highest mountain in Pakistan. He has a vision like the great men I mentioned who have changed history. He is relaxed. He is confident in everything he says and does. He is short, but walks tall. He knows how to laugh. He is firm and purposeful. He exudes strength. He leads the people where they want to go. He will give our boy a sense of glory about himself, the kind of confidence he lacks and needs to compete in this world."

He paused. His eyes turned to Lois and he softly said, "Does that answer your question my dear wife?"

The look on her husband's face told Lois that the issue was a settled one, and further discussion would not be welcome. Deep inside her she was overcome with a feeling of foreboding, but she had to say one thing more, "But you never answered my question" she pleaded softly.

"It has been answered," he whispered.

CHAPTER 6

RUSSIA

Anatoly Shenko:

Novosibirsk, Siberia is a prominent city lying along the Ob River in Western Siberia. The winters are cold and snowy and the summers are hot and dry. There is plenty of sun even during the winter months, and the temperature differences between summer and winter are extreme, one of the highest on the European and Asian continents. The city boasts of its opera and ballet companies, theaters, art galleries, and numerous Russian Olympians, most notably Alexander Karelin, the nine time Greco-Roman wrestling world champion (including three Olympic gold medals). It is also the home of some of Russia's finest universities and scientific research centers.

The scientific complex known as Gradient is located forty kilometers southeast of Novosobirsk, the site of the Siberian branch of the Russian Academy of Science. Gradient has eighty labs and administrative buildings. In the basement of building 42 are well-guarded, isolated virology-research laboratories devoted to the development of virus weapons of mass destruction. In the adjacent building 43, and connected by secret tunnel, is another basement facility devoted to the development of bacteriological weapons of mass destruction: anthrax and bubonic plague.

Efforts to aerosolize these biological weapons and make them transportable without mitigating their lethal potential finally met success after several years of work.

Not long after the Soviet Union collapsed, Iran began recruiting Gradient's premier scientists and administrative officers with the idea of developing state-of-the-art biological warfare capabilities. However, the United States has a stake in Gradient's invulnerability, so together with the Russians they worked to make the Russian facility, and their own, impervious to the possibility of theft. The best American-made cameras and motion sensors, plus a triple layer of visible and invisible fences now surround both facilities in Russia and the United States. The facilities are as invulnerable as human beings can make them.

Gradient is equipped with a negative pressure ventilation system so there is no chance of viral or bacterial contamination reaching the outside world. The entrances and exits are hermetically sealed. Wastewater, decontamination suits and instruments receive treatment at temperatures sure to destroy any viral or bacterial pathogens. The power supply has a double foolproof back up system.

Sixty-one year old Anatoly Shenko had started working in Novosibirsk ever since he obtained his Ph.D. in microbiology from Rostov University at the age of twenty-five. After twelve years of research in Novosibirsk's main virology facility, he went to Gradient where he worked on top-secret biological warfare: anthrax and small pox. He became one of the leading experts in his field and obtained the highest level of security clearance.

Anthrax is one of the diseases of antiquity. Some consider it to have been the cause of the fifth and sixth plague of Exodus. It is the first disease proven to result from infectious bacteria.

Louis Pasteur developed the first antibacterial vaccine in history against anthrax. The illness comes from *Bacillus anthracis* whose two protein toxins can cause severe symptoms, or lead to death. Three forms of the disease exist: cutaneous anthrax causes a severe localized infection of the skin; gastrointestinal anthrax develops from the ingestion of contaminated meat; inhalation anthrax can cause disease on inhalation of the bacteria. This latter form has the greatest potential for biological terrorism.

Bacillus anthracis is a spore-forming organism. The spores can become inactive and non-infectious when deprived of certain nutrients, or subjected to adverse environmental conditions. They have hibernated, so to speak, or developed a state of suspended animation. In this form, they can survive in the soil for decades. If inhaled by man, the spores will then find themselves surrounded by the proper environment and necessary nutrients. Then within sixty days, the spores will come to life. Unless treated early this illness is fatal.

Anatoly Shenko developed the procedure for reducing the anthrax bacillus to its smallest spore form, thus realizing the potential for a very effective and easy to disseminate aerosolized agent.

The other biological weapon that Shenko worked with was smallpox. In ancient times, this scourge could decimate a town, at times killing fifty percent of a population as well as scarring many for life.

An effective vaccination technique throughout the world has eliminated smallpox as a threat. Therefore, for over forty years, no one has received vaccination. The smallpox virus that has been stored in four laboratories around the world is available in case it should ever be necessary to make vaccine. This could be the source for bio-terrorism if the samples are not well controlled, and one of these storage laboratories was Gradient where Anatoly Shenko did his pioneering work in biological warfare. Smallpox virus is the ideal biological warfare agent as it disseminates in the air when aerosolized.

Anatoly Shenko was quiet and reserved. He was devoted to his work. His sedentary existence working in his administrative office and his laboratory bench resulted in his gaining weight over the years. He was a short man, now almost as wide as he was tall. He had male pattern baldness, with hair present only above his ears and the back of his head. In all the years he had worked in this risky environment, he was one of the few who managed never to become infected with the organism they were working with. He attributed this to never taking for granted the strict safety measures that he, as chairperson of the safety committee, had developed.

Anatoly was married with four children including one mentally and physically retarded son whose constant care and expense took a toll on him as well as his wife and family.

Growing up under the Soviet Communist system, Anatoly was a card-carrying Communist, but never made the money or had the benefits that upper echelon Communist political bosses received. When the Soviet Union collapsed, embittered by his personal plight, Anatoly breathed a sigh of relief. However, over time, conditions did not change for him and his family.

He worked late one evening in order to prepare another batch of smallpox virus to be stored. In reality, however, he had a plan to obtain a good supply of the virus and the anthrax spores and smuggle them out of the country. He was getting older. His health was poor. How much longer would he be around? His wife was also in poor health. Her physical difficulties, complicated by significant worry over her disabled son added up to a chronic depression. Anatoly would not go to his grave without arranging for the long term care of his son that would not include institutionalization. He had made all arrangements. He was content.

After the threat of smallpox ended, the international community agreed that rather than destroy all smallpox virus remaining, they would keep enough for purposes of research or vaccine development. In Russia, this was his domain.

CHAPTER 7

CHECHNYA

Abdul Saididov:

Abdul Saidadov was born and raised in Moscow. His parents had moved to Russia from the Nausky district of Chechnya so his father could take on a temporary teaching assignment at Moscow University. As a child, he and his parents would spend much of the summer in Chechnya's mountainous terrain where they kept a small home. The rest of the year, he lived and studied in Russia.

Abdul was educated at the University of Moscow as a bacteriologist and virologist. He had spent much time training in other Russian locations and in Siberia. He then returned to Chechnya to head the microbiology department in the largest hospital in the Nausky district.

Abdul's parents moved back to Chechnya, and after the collapse of the Soviet Union, they became leaders in the Chechnya struggle to free themselves from Russian dominance. The Russians would have none of it. They fought against the Chechen rebels with military and economic force. They convinced Iran not to provide support for the rebels who were Muslim zealots bent on overthrowing Russian control of their country and establish an Islamic republic. For this, Iran would get favored nation status including assistance in the development of nuclear power. This interested the Iranians who had hopes of developing the nuclear bomb and becoming a great regional and world power.

When Abdul's parents were killed in the struggle, a grieving Abdul took up arms where his parents had left off, and he did so with a hate that consumed and changed him. His initial goal—to which he devoted much of his adulthood—was to create an independent Chechen state, but he could only stand by in frustration as the Russians repressed the rebellion. Embittered, he had chosen another route. He realized that the battle against the Russians was too narrow in focus. As a dedicated Islamist, he now had greater goals, and he met them by an alliance with al Qaeda. This posture alienated him from some of his former Chechen allies, but the few that agreed with him dedicated their life to the greater struggle: the one for world dominance under the rule of Allah.

When the fighting stopped, Abdul returned to the microbiological arena, but he no longer focused on patient care and diagnosis. His outlook had become broader, more global in scope. He would now focus on his area of expertise, virology and bacteriology and their use to advance the cause of global religious war.

Abdul was a large man for a Chechen. Slightly over six feet in height, he made an imposing figure with a neat, black beard graying at the sides of his chin in sharp contrast to his thick, disheveled eyebrows, angling up at the periphery, giving him a devilish appearance. He was ruggedly handsome with a wind and sunburned face. A large frame, none of it due to fat, added to the impression of power. He had respect for others of his own ilk, was faithful to his God, but his wartime exploits had made him a heartless killer. Orders were never questioned, but were carried out less grave consequences be suffered. He still knew Anatoly Shenko with whom he had kept in close contact. Anatoly had the power to make him an important force in the global religious war. He had worked with him in microbiology labs in and around Moscow, in Novosibirsk, and in Gradient. With the changes in the former Soviet Union, Anatoly, always underpaid and under great personal pressure, was desperate to make a living. What he needed was money. What Abdul needed was money. With this in mind, Abdul set out for Waziristan, and his contacts took him to the man himself: Ayman Zawalacki.

A group of masked men armed with Kalashnikoff rifles and grenade launchers met Abdul. His companions were told to go back home. The men took a blindfolded Abdul over mountainous terrain. When they arrived at their destination, they removed his blindfold. He sat on a large square rug, blinked to clear his sight and he saw the same armed masked men standing at his sides. He recognized the men he had come to see, sitting on the other side of the rug.

As he looked, he thought. So these are the men who sent a message in blood to the United States, the Great Satan; these are the men who bring Islam to the entire world. They resembled their pictures except for more gray in their beards. Allah had blessed him.

They feasted and spoke, and three days later, he was back in Chechnya with a promise and a warning. The promise—that an Imam with two chipped front teeth would deliver the money to Abdul and pick up the promised packages from Abdul. The warning—that his life would be forfeit if he reneged on the delivery of what he had promised.

The meeting took place in the same cave Abdul had found when he was a child playing in the mountains. The entrance to the cave was invisible to any one of the rare villagers who happened to pass by, but if they knew where the hidden tiny entrance was, they could crawl for fifteen meters and then enter a large room with a high ceiling. The room was circular in shape with a diameter of approximately six meters, furnished only with a large square oriental rug bequeathed to Abdul by his father. It was right that the type of meetings held here played out on his father's gift, for his father had also been a dedicated Islamist, and Abdul had learned of Allah on his father's knee. This room was where he would hold secret meetings away from the prowling eyes of his enemies. Here is where he met with the Imam with the chipped front teeth, and the Imam's small band of believers who had come all the way from the Pakistan-Afghanistan border. The Imam passed the money to Abdul who in turn passed it to a shadowy round figure with his face draped like a woman who arrived before the Imam had. For this, they received two large boxes, climate controlled, well insulated and heavy. The Imam and his entourage took the boxes and left. The round figure took his money and left.

Abdul smiled at the ease of the operation. He had been the transfer agent. He was content, for he played a major role in the great global religious war for world control. Soon there would be a decisive blow for Allah struck in that war.

CHAPTER 8

PAKISTAN

The Imam:

"Yes, Ben, that is right. The Koran forbids suicide." The Imam paused. He looked at Ben sitting in silence. This was an important day in the learning process. His student, Ben Marzan, an American citizen, needed careful handling. He was the perfect candidate. He was born of an American mother, who had converted to Islam, and a Muslim father. Ben had grown to manhood in the United States, therefore was already assimilated into the culture; and for the assigned task, this assimilation was the principle requirement.

The plan was that Ben, after a year of indoctrination, would go back home to the United States, and join three others as a group of Trojan Horses and live in the Chicago area where Ben planned to go to school. Only these Trojan Horses would be different from the Trojan Horse as told in Virgil's Latin poem epic, The Aenid. Their goal would not be to capture a city, but rather to destroy a city—and that city was Chicago picked as the next target in the great global religious war. The city, a major rail, air hub, and financial center was perfect. Americans would be expecting another attack on New York or Washington, D.C. Ben would be one of the avenging angels. He would be welcomed back in his country. Soon after, the Great Satan would know he had returned.

Ben and the Imam sat cross-legged on a rug facing each other. They were the only ones in the office, a small 10 by 10 feet room with a circular oriental rug and six pillows. Ben's dark brown eyes stared at his Imam teacher. Behind the Imam, and facing Ben, was a small bookcase filled with Pashto language books and the Koran. The Koran, held upright by golden eagle-shaped bookends, stood by itself in the center of one of the shelves at eye level to a seated Ben.

Ben's pitch-black beard hid his mouth under the growth and betrayed the fact that he was eighteen years old. His bright eyes shone forth like twin lighthouse beacons from above his beard and from under his turban. He was clothed in a long cloth, mantle and baggy pants. He was ready for prayer.

The Imam, dressed in similar garb, was fifty-five years old. He had a bulbous nose, a black mustache, pointed at the ends, and a long salt-and-pepper beard. His fingers were thin and tapered and they danced in the air as he spoke. When he read from the Koran, his right index finger, never touching the pages, pointed to what he was reading. When he was not quoting or reading from the book, his fingers drummed on the floor adjacent to the rug. Even when he was not speaking, his hands were in motion. He read every word from the book with a booming voice, each word enunciated with devotion. Normal conversation, not involving the book, was spoken in a quieter voice forcing Ben to extreme attentiveness less he might misunderstand the Imam's words. Several of the Imam's front teeth chipped as the result of a fall on a mountain climbing expedition, he left as proof that appearance was unimportant in a world where dedication to Allah meant everything. The Imam stared at his pupil and smiled. He knew: Ben's mind and body had been receptive. He was a quick learner.

"If you look at statistics, Ben, you would learn that suicide is a rare occurrence in Muslim society." He choose to speak to his student in perfect English, the birth language of Ben's mother, rather than Pashto, the language, less familiar to Ben, of his father, Hari, born and reared with the tribes of Northwest Pakistan. "Suicide is a major sin. The Koran says, 'Do not kill yourself, for if you do you will be cast into the fire and cannot go to paradise.'"

Ben did not speak. He continued to stare into the eyes of his Imam. The Imam stared back. "But there is a difference, Ben, between suicide and martyrdom." The Imam paused again. He closed his eyes and raised his arms, his fingers moving in ecstatic motion. "For martyrdom is not suicide, but rather it is a self sacrifice when done for Holy War to please Allah, and he who performs martyrdom in the name of Holy War will win the eternal gratefulness of Allah, and eternal affection from the beautiful maidens in paradise. Plus, and I stress this, you receive eternal knowledge. You will understand the mind of God. You see, Ben, when you attack the enemy and die, you strike a blow for Allah and put fear and terror in the hearts of the oppressors. There is no greater homage that can be paid to Allah."

"Yes," said Ben with quiet passion, his eyes staring into the Imam's face.

"Our enemies have precision weapons, Ben, the so called 'smart bomb,' a bomb that can be directed with great accuracy to a target. As good as those are, they are not as precise as our own precision weapon, our own smart bomb—the suicide bomber. Here you're talking precision in millimeters. What could be more precise than one dedicated to Allah intent on a target that he or she walks to? Let the great Satan spend the billions on the high-tech armaments. We counter with martyrdom.

"Our enemies are certain that technology would dominate the twenty-first century. They feel that their armaments will lead them to world-control, but they are wrong. We will be led to dominance by our Holy Martyrs, and all they need is a few pounds of explosives wrapped around their bodies with a detonator that once they press will propel them to paradise for all eternity. This weapon of ours, Ben, is in its early stages of development today, but we are planning for the time when our martyrs will strike in waves like the blitzkrieg of World War II. Yes, God is great," said a contented Imam.

He felt he had made much headway with Ben. This represented a year of work as opposed to the time it took to develop a martyr from kindergarten. Five-year olds are the Holy Martyrs of tomorrow. There the work was easy. You took a young child's mind, filled it with hatred for the enemy, nurtured this mindset and soon you had grown men ready to be Holy Martyrs. It was like growing a plant from the planting of the seed to careful fertilization and watering. When the plants grow up, they flower into a Holy Martyr. In Ben's case, he had watched the power of Allah transition Ben from an irritable, confused youngster to a dedicated Islamist and Holy Warrior.

"Our enemies have nuclear bombs, Ben. We counter with a more powerful method, human bombs."

The Imam sighed. His present student was the ideal candidate: he had learned to manifest an intense love for Islam, and he had no criminal record. He was an unknown. The perfect innocent. He was beyond suspicion. "It is time, Ben. It is not heroic. It is holy. God is Great."

"Uh-huh, God is Great," answered Ben.

"We are at a time in our history when the pagans are attacking Muslims all over the world. It is time to unite under Allah's banner. We must fight and kill the infidels wherever we find them. The Prophet Muhammad said, "I was ordered to fight all men until they say, there is no God but Allah. We must never forget the tragedy of al-Andalus. Our obligation is to convert everybody to Islam. That is our Islamic mission, Ben.

"You will be a true Holy Warrior. The United States leads the pagans in a crusade to use Allah's holy lands as a beachhead to reach out and enslave other Muslim lands. The crusaders and the Zionists together have united to conquer Jerusalem. The Americans and the Israelis are a single two-headed coin. The Americans use Israel in a plot against Islam. To assure that the world only worships Allah, we go with the sword in our hands. The crimes of the United States and their allies demand a religious ruling. It is the duty of all Muslims to kill Americans and their allies, wherever we find them. Do you understand, Ben?"

"Yes, I do Imam."

"Good, You are perfect for us. You are very intelligent and you are an excellent learner. As you adopt our philosophy, you will see that your understanding of everything becomes clearer. Have you noticed the ease by which your advanced mathematics sticks in your brain, Ben?"

"Yes, I do, Imam."

"The more that you accept our way of thought, the easier it will be to comprehend mathematics. That is a guarantee. It would be an honor to have you join us, Ben. We are The Trojan Horses, the Takfirs. We are the only true sect. Our way is the only possible way to a world of Allah."

"Do you understand what The Trojan Horses mean, Ben?"

"I think so, Imam."

"It means we infiltrate and assimilate in the land of our enemies. We blend in. We are beyond suspicion. We are each a Trojan Horse; a Trojan

Horse in a foreign land, but our Trojan horses make the Trojan Horse in the Aenid look like an ant next to an elephant. Our Trojan Horses will not conquer a city, they will change a world, and you, Ben, will lead the way. Our enemies welcome us; we are to them as one, and as we are welcomed, we will conquer for they have no idea as to our ultimate goal. We will restore the Islamic Empire. We will go back to the days of glory when our Islamic political empire controlled the entire Middle East. Fifty years after that, we will have the entire world. Think on that, Ben."

Ben nodded and smiled—a closed mouth closed eyed smile.

"Do you accept The Assimilated philosophy, Ben?"

"I do, Imam," he said with eyes still closed.

"Then you are exempt from Islamic law. Do you understand why?"

"Yes, I must appear entirely secular so as to blend in."

"Yes, that is correct. It will be easy for you. You are already an American. You are a Trojan Horse already born in a foreign land that we will change. Oh, if we had a thousand just like you we could conquer the world in short order. That goal is only possible through violent struggle, and we will be successful. Allah has directed us. We can not fail."

"I understand, Imam."

"We infiltrate enemy societies, and we take any measure necessary to accomplish this goal. You are perfect for us now, as you have embraced the philosophy. Your outward appearance will be complete secular assimilation, but on the inside, the idea of religious war will never leave your mind and will be foremost in your thoughts. Anyone, including Muslims, who offer the slightest opposition to our mission can and must be done away with. Do you understand, Ben?"

"Yes, Imam."

"Remember what I say here today. Once you are in, there is no turning back You are a member forever."

"Yes, Imam."

"Good, Are you ready?"

"Yes, I am ready," smiled Ben.

"When you go to school in Chicago, you will be clean shaven. You'll wear your American clothes, get rid of your ponytail, resume your American name, start school and take a part time job where you can mix with hundreds of people. Then you will go to meet Steve. You will only know his first name, and he will only know you as Ben. He will be your contact. He too is a Trojan Horse, only he was not born there like you. He was sent there and has gone to school there and lives and works among the people. There are more. Steve will have your picture from your high school yearbook. He lives in Chicago at 2789 Addison Avenue on the third floor. If you go there any weekday at six o'clock in the evening, he will be there. You will never call him by wire phone or cell phone. You will never write him notes or send letters or emails. We have a cell in Chicago. They do not congregate in their homes. They have ways of communicating with each other that you will learn when you get there. They have been in place for a long time. They have great weapons for the struggle. We are counting on them. Now you will be a part of what we consider the greatest operation in the history of Islam. Go with Allah, Ben."

CHAPTER 9

Back home:

Ben went back to his temporary residence. He calmly shaved, cut off his ponytail and got a short haircut. His life had a purpose. Everything he did now would be with that purpose in mind. This last year had been an incredible learning experience. His father had sent him to a holy man with whom he had spent an entire year and had learned what life meant; that happiness comes from serving humanity. True it would be a long struggle, but the result would be a paradise here on earth—an earth no longer held back by the infidels. This was now the purpose of his existence. Everything else he would do would be to prepare for the struggle.

Of great help to him in this task was mathematics. He had finished all of high school mathematics through calculus by the end of his sophomore year. He could have taken more through a local college, but he had chosen not to do so. Rather, he self learned from his father's math texts that filled the library in their Madison home. He would try to study whenever he could, but the cloud and the fire that would return often prevented him from full concentration on this task—but no longer. Now that he had learned from the Imam how to control these beasts by study and concentration on Allah, he could keep his mind from straying from the most important task—Holy War. He knew when to concentrate on difficult math problems in order to prevent his mind from turning inward. This would never happen anymore thanks to the Imam. Dealing with these math problems dissipated the clouds and quenched the fire. They had now become even easier to solve. A Trojan horse could never deviate from the task. It was too important. This is how it worked. He knew what to do. He would not fail.

Ben's father knew that his son was changing. He could tell by the weekly letters and by the occasional phone call, and when he saw Ben in person stepping from the plane at O'Hare Field, he knew what his instinct had told him. His son had indeed changed. This had been a great year. The Imam had worked his magic.

Ben's mother, Lois, saw the same change in her son. She was overwhelmed. His ponytail was gone. His hair was combed and short. His face reflected a calmness and maturity that she had never seen before. It was as if another son had been born. How was it possible to change so? She prayed and hoped for the best.

Ben's parents drove from O'Hare field back to Madison. Ben was silent and spoke only when his parents spoke to him. On the way home, Hari said, "You look good, Ben. I see calmness in your eyes. You are a changed man. Are you satisfied with your experience with the Imam?"

"I am, father. I understand what my problem was and now I know how to control it. I'm anxious to start school."

"Have you decided on a major?" asked Hari as Lois listened with interest.

"Mathematics. I've learned how to use math to control my emotions, and my mind is clearer and much more focused."

"That's very good," said Hari with a contented smile on his face. "How do you mean?"

"Math seems to level my brain and keep me on an even keel. It forces me to concentrate and it stabilizes my mood. It even can change me. Once I had a bad toothache, and it was late at night, so I put my attention to a LaPlace Transform problem and worked all night on it. The next thing I knew it was seven in the morning, and I realized that I had spent the whole night concentrating and did not feel pain."

"What was wrong with your tooth?" asked Lois in alarm.

"The Imam had a dentist see me and he couldn't find anything wrong, so he changed the filling in that tooth and it worked. I had no more pain."

"Oh, that's good," said Lois.

"I'm not surprised to hear that," said Hari. There is nothing that could absorb a mind like a tough math problem."

They arrived at their Madison home. Ben stared at its opulence, a thought that had never entered his mind before he left for his yearlong session with the Imam. His home was in sharp contrast to the simple surroundings of his quarters in Pakistan. Living here with his mother and father had been the quintessential assimilation in the land of the infidel. It had worked its magic. Ben and the Imam would both be pleased.

The Marzan home was a tri-level on a side street, built in the shape of a cube with a three-car garage adjacent to the left side of the house as you approached it from the front. You entered into a handsome foyer, and off to the left was a square shaped dining room. To the right was a rectangular shaped living room. Also on the main floor was a kitchen, dining area, bathroom and family room with a home entertainment center. Directly ahead was a winding staircase leading up to the second level where there were four bedrooms, two bathrooms and a study. The basement level was made into a large recreation room with a library, family room furnishings and a three-cushioned billiard table. It was here that Hari had taught Ben geometry and trigonometry while studying billiard ball ricochets. Ben's room was just the way he had left it. Lois had seen to that.

"Look in the garage," said Hari.

To Ben's surprise, there were three cars. "I can't believe it," exclaimed Ben with a smile on his face. "Is one for me?" he asked with a degree of trepidation.

"Yes of course," said Hari. "You'll need your own transportation now to travel back home and visit your parents."

CHAPTER 10

CHICAGO

Steve:

Ben settled in to his new living accommodations in one of the dormitories at Northwestern University. He had much to do. Soon he would start school and get a part time evening job where he would meet people.

He was following all the Imam's recommendations. What better way to assimilate than be a typical student, work part time to make some money for expenses and be one of the boys. He had an important secret he had to keep from them.

He took a job working three evenings per week five to nine at a McDonald's not far from the campus. Once settled in on his new job he would visit Steve for instructions. According to the Imam, Steve would be home every night this week waiting for a visit from his new Trojan Horse.

He drove down Sheridan Road to Lake Shore Drive to Addison Ave and parked on the 2700 block. He found a large apartment building shaped like a U with two entrances on each long leg of the U. He found the 2789 entrance, walked up to the third floor and knocked on the door. A stern-looking man peeked out through the opening. He smiled when he saw Ben, released the latch, and opened the door.

"You must be Steve," said Ben.

"Yes, Ben, that's my name. Come in."

Ben entered and walked into a small living room furnished with a small television set, a couch, a rectangular end table and a large recliner opposite the TV.

Off to the right was a small bathroom and bedroom. Adjacent to the living room was a dining room furnished with a bookcase, a large table and four chairs. Off to the right of the dining room was a standing-room-only kitchen.

Steve was of medium height about one inch shorter than Ben, had a dark complexion, and wore glasses with thick lenses. His hair was black and wavy. "Sit at the head of the table while I get the supplies," said Steve.

The Imam told him that Steve would be in charge, and Ben was to follow all instructions without question. It was clear to Ben that Steve was indeed a take-charge person and he spoke in a confident and firm voice. Ben watched and wondered what supplies Steve was talking about as he watched Steve walk to the kitchen and open the refrigerator. He took out a small metal box and brought it to the dining room table. "All the Trojan Horses have been vaccinated, Ben. You're the last one and then we'll be ready."

Ben nodded. Now he knew.

"We're having a hot summer. I would vaccinate you on the upper arm, but that could become too obvious. I don't want to force you to have to wear long sleeves, so I'll use the upper, outer part of your thigh. You're going to need full use of your arms with the job we've got to do. Lower your pants and stand here next to me," said Steve.

Ben complied and Steve continued, "Let me tell you what I'm doing, Ben. First of all, the vaccine is not a smallpox virus vaccine. It's made from a virus called Vaccinia, which is related to the smallpox virus called Variola. I'm about to give you a live Vaccinia virus and it'll make you immune to smallpox. The immunity will last about five years and you will not have to worry about catching the disease like the infidels will when we introduce it to them.

There are two more Trojan Horses you haven't met, Ben. You're the fourth. We will spread the smallpox virus to the good citizens of Chicago, Ben. We'll stop the city dead in its tracks. God is Great. You will not be involved in this action, Ben, but you will be protected like the rest of us when we give the infidels their gift.

"God is Great," answered a smiling Ben wondering how many and where were the other Trojan Horses?

Ben watched as Steve opened the metal box and took out a two-pronged needle. He then dipped the needle into a liquid held in a small vial. Ben could see that the needle held a drop of the liquid between its two prongs. He watched as Steve used the needle and pricked him multiple times on the lateral aspect of his left thigh. Two small droplets of blood formed and Steve said, "That's all there is to it. In a few days, you'll see an itchy red bump. Don't scratch it, you don't want to irritate it and get it infected. Just do some gentle padding if the itch gets too bothersome. Got that, Ben?"

"I got it."

"Then it'll form a blister and fill with some fluid that will drain a little. By the second week, you'll develop a scab that'll fall off in three or four days. It'll leave a scar, and that'll be the sign you're protected, Ben. Wear the scar proudly; it's your mark from Allah that means you are one of the chosen ones."

Ben nodded. "I understand," said a smiling Ben.

Steve took another vial out of the box and said, "Now I will give you an anthrax immunization shot, Ben. I'll give you two more in the next two weeks. Then we'll be ready."

CHAPTER 11

Sami Ghattara:

Steve Gilbert, formerly known as Sami Ghattara, was born in Lebanon and travelled to the United States to live with relatives and attend high school. Prior to his leaving he was indoctrinated by his father, a prominent Hizbollah Imam. The indoctrination centered on the fact that Israel must cease to exist, and one of the best ways to accomplish this goal is to immobilize the United States. It was all part of the Great Global Religious War to make the Great Satan impotent.

Steve had become a United States citizen during his senior year in college. He graduated from the University of Chicago as an architect, and worked for a downtown firm. He went to Loyola University at night and earned an MBA. He assimilated into American Society very well. He spoke English with a Chicago accent; the deez, dem and doze made for a perfect assimilation.

He had paid close attention to the United States mindset, and he knew that the majority of people in the country did not feel as he and his fellow Holy Warriors felt—that the United States was now engaging Allah in a World War. The average American citizen was too busy worrying about domestic and economic issues to think much about terrorist attacks on their country any more. The horror of 9-11 was slowly dissipating.

In terms of long term planning, Steve had been disappointed at the 9-11 strike. He felt that with the lax immigration policy of the United States before 9-11, it would have been better to continue the policy of immigration and assimilation when it was easier to do so. Then when the time came, they would have had thousands of assimilated Trojan Horses ready to strike as one all over the country. He felt that this would render the

United States helpless, the victim of 1000 Pearl Harbors, or 1000 World Trade Centers all occurring in one day.

With the 9-11 strike, the leadership of the United States had struck back with its armed might, with money, and with its emotion. Steve was disappointed because he felt that this action set back their timetable. On the other hand, the eventual ever-increasing skepticism of the average U. S. citizen about their government's policy and the naiveté of the world community over the threat of world terrorism was an encouraging sign.

He and his American Trojan Horses, and other assimilated associates had no choice but to keep up the struggle and nibble away at the Great Satan. It could take one hundred years, but victory was certain. There were many ways to do damage, and Steve's responsibility involved directing a simultaneous organized biological attack on the city of Chicago with further instructions to follow. This project would require careful planning, and the Imam had noted Steve's educational background and managerial expertise and rewarded him with the leadership of this great and holy task.

Steve and two others divided the city and suburbs. Once Ben completed the immunizations, he would be the last chip to fall into place. Then three of the Trojan horses, not including Ben, would act in unison according to a well thought out plan, and render the city helpless. There was more to come. When Ben inquired as to the nature of the "more to come," he received a one word answer—"patience, that's where you come in, Ben." With that one word, Ben new better than to make further inquiries, but wondered as to the "That's where you come in, Ben."

Steve laughed aloud as he thought of American preparations for BioShield, a concept introduced by the U. S. president in a State of the Union speech made before congress. He had asked for six billion dollars to finance the project that would "make available effective vaccines and treatments against agents like Anthrax, Botulinum Toxin, Ebola and Plague. Steve noticed that smallpox was never mentioned, no doubt because the powers to be were lulled into a false sense of security over the fact that the disease of smallpox had been wiped off the face of the earth. Most citizens did not know that the only stores of smallpox virus remaining, locked up in vaults in secure labs in four countries of the world, was available only for special research and emergencies. Steve had access to the virus, and the anthrax spores. He received them from a man he had never seen before, and with that gift went formal instruction in its dissemination and use. He had made the mistake of asking how they got the virus, and they told him that such information is of no concern to him. As a loyal Trojan Horse, Steve was to carry out orders, and his orders were to be sure that the orders he was given by his superiors were carried out—"to the letter," as the Infidels say.

Steve smiled at the perfection of the organization of which he was a part. To think of the amazing planning and coordination that must have gone into the acquiring of the deadly smallpox virus and anthrax spores. The smile turned into another laugh as he thought about how the American federal bureaucracy botched BioShield. The larger pharmaceutical firms had no interest in developing bio-defense medications, nor did they have any interest in the development of vaccines and face the mountains of litigation that would be sure to follow. How naïve the President of the United States was to think that the BioShield program would attract companies submitting bids for contracts from the government. He had read that with the pharmaceutical industries' profits facing downward pressures, the last thing they wanted to do was work on BioShield. Their interest was in the development of blockbuster drugs. That was what drove up their stock price. Capitalism was working in terrorism's favor.

It was true that the government had stock piled 300,000,000 doses of smallpox vaccine, and had awarded a contract to a small company to develop 75,000,000 doses of anthrax vaccine, however, the small company had not completed its task. The plan Steve had responsibility for implementing in Chicago, would sweep like a hurricane through the city, and, before the authorities realized what was happening, tens of thousands would die. The health, educational and economic consequences would be devastating. The beauty of it all was that Chicago and the state of Illinois received recognition as two of the best-prepared sites in the nation to handle a biological warfare attack. What a surprise was awaiting them. One of the reasons they chose Chicago was to show that even the best Chicago preparation was for naught. Also it was expected that the terrorists would attack New York or Washington D.C.; so why not another big city? Anything was possible. Steve knew that the time to strike was approaching soon. Then it was up to him to mobilize his team to strike in a well-timed, cohesive manner—and bring Chicago to its knees.

CHAPTER 12

CHICAGO

Amanda Galinski M.D. Jason Pollard M.D.

Amanda Galinski M.D., a recent graduate of the University of Illinois College of Medicine, entered the Emergency Department of Covenant Hospital for her first day on duty. Two years ago, she had spent three months there as a medical student working under the tutelage of Dr. Jason Pollard, chairperson of Emergency Medicine. She was now starting the first day of a three-year stint as an emergency medicine resident physician. During the time she would call this home, she hoped to transition from an inexperienced novice to a polished emergency physician capable of handling the great variety of medical problems that walk, or are carried through Covenant's doors. Although, as Pollard had told her, "After three months as a clinical clerk, four years as a medical student and three years as a resident, you'll realize that the true learning process will just begin; you'll be prepared to learn for the rest of your life. Hardly a day goes by when you will not experience something new that you either have never heard of or have never seen before. That is why you are a constant learner. That is why you must remain a student all your practice life."

As she walked through the rear doors of the Emergency Department, she wanted to savor the moment she had been dreaming about ever since she worked as a sixteen-year old candy-striper at Resurrection Hospital not far from the Chicago home where she was raised. She stopped and looked at the large rectangular shaped main section of the Emergency Department with its ten rooms on each long end of the rectangle. A flood of memories returned as she scrutinized each of the twenty rooms. There's where she saw patient X. What a learning experience that was. Patient Y in room twelve was where she saw all the clinical manifestations of congestive heart failure. Room fourteen—the failed attempt to revive the cardiac arrest. Room eight—the beautiful three-year-old boy who, without a sound or a tear, sat through the repair of a large laceration on his arm. Tears came to her eyes. The three months she had spent here in her medical school junior clerkship had been the highlight of her embryonic medical career.

She looked with fond and not so fond memories at the inner rectangle of the Emergency Department where the doctors and nurses carried out much of the documenting, thinking and studying.

The nursing station was located in this area. Amanda remembered the time she spent there talking to other physicians, charting, using the telephone, retrieving supplies, checking medical textbooks, looking up medications in the Physicians Desk Reference and just sitting and relaxing when patient volume diminished.

Her right hand reached into her light-blue lab coat pocket and took out some tissue. She dabbed the tears from her large, brown eyes. She forced a smile to bring herself back to reality, and her white teeth sparkled like a toothpaste advertisement. She was a trim five feet six inches tall. She wore white slacks and a white blouse under her lab coat. She cut her hair short as a compromise to the hectic nature of her new career. Her identification tag, attached to the upper right pocket of her lab coat said 'she was ready."

She saw Gail Cowen, the director of nursing in the Emergency Department, engaged in charting at the nursing station. "Good morning, Ms. Cowen," Amanda said.

Cowen looked up over her reading glasses. She rose from the chair her full five feet eleven inch height, smiled, and extended her hand. "Amanda, I mean Dr. Galinski." Her smile broadened. "This is your first day, and we're so glad to have you here."

"And I'm so glad to be here," said Amanda grasping her hand.

"Dr. Pollard got here about fifteen minutes ago. He's in his office waiting for you."

Amanda's head turned in the direction of Pollard's office, a worried look on her face. "Oh, I hope I'm not late."

"No, you're early as a matter of fact. You'll learn that Dr. Pollard is always here about fifteen minutes early. He told me to send you to his office when you got here. Just go right in."

Pollard's office, situated ten yards from the rear entrance to the Emergency Department was a model of convenience. The door was open and she walked in, but Pollard was not there. It was almost two years since she had been in his office. It might have been yesterday, because not a thing had changed. The large L-shaped desk was where it had always been—in front of the built-in bookcases on the back wall. On the desk were the usual documents and charts. The picture of Pollard and his family was on the same corner of the desk. Photographed about five years ago Pollard was standing, his trim six foot three inch height dominant on the photograph. He had a crooked smile. Amanda noted there was an expression on Dr. Pollard's face that reminded her of a small boy just caught with his hand in the cookie jar. His brown hair had a touch of a wave. His beautiful wife, Sarah, was at his side, the top of her head just above her husband's shoulder. Six children stood three on each side smiling the smile of the photographer asking them to say cheese. On the short L of the desk was the same computer that she remembered, and behind the desk on the top shelf was the row of books in every specialty, including some new ones she didn't recall seeing before. She remembered often what Pollard had told her. "An emergency medicine physician has to learn to speak the language of all the specialists." On the next shelf were the last four years of Emergency Medicine journals. In front of the desk was the same couch and matching chairs that she recalled sitting on during her clinical rotation as a junior medical student. She shook her head and noticed a water cooler in the corner. That wasn't here then, she thought. She sat down on the couch, sighed and waited, her eyes closed, her mind fighting off memories, but full of anticipation.

When Pollard walked back in the room, Amanda didn't hear him. Pollard sat down and looked at her closed eyes. "Tired, Amanda?" he said

Her head shot up. Her eyes opened. She sat upright. "Oh no," she said, "Just thinking."

"I can imagine," said Pollard. "What were you thinking about?"

"Just remembering my past experience here during my clerkship and now anticipating the future," she sighed.

"Good, Amanda, when one starts a residency with such anticipation you're off to a good start."

"Thank you. I'll give it my all."

"I know you will. You'll work with me the first three months. The other residents are assigned other attending physicians. Once a week we'll all get together for a meeting to discuss clinical and quality issues, and once a month we'll have a department meeting. None of that has changed since you were a student here. I hope you had a chance to read the Emergency Department Manual. Every so often I may hit you with a surprise question."

"I'll be ready, Dr. Pollard."

"We're equal Amanda. Your doctor degree is now official. So at a time like this I'm Jason and you're Amanda. In front of the patients, I'm Dr. Pollard and you're Dr. Galinski. Remember what we agreed upon when you were a junior clerk?"

"How can I ever forget, Jason."

"Let's get to work, Amanda."

CHAPTER 13

Small Pox:

"We've got one item on the agenda this morning, and that's to learn about smallpox and our policies to be prepared in the event of a bio-terrorist attack. Okay let's get on to business. A quick sidelight first that will sort-of tell what we're up against. When I graduated medical school in 1995, the hospital still had a ninety-two-year-old doctor on the staff. His name was Zakon, and if he was ninety-two in 1995, he was born in 1903. He was a brand new doctor in 1927, and took further training in dermatology in Vienna. That is what they did in those days before we had residencies. You studied in Vienna, Austria or Berlin, Germany, and voila, you were a specialist. Those were the micas of medical learning back then. Anyhow, he came back to the United States and became a world famous dermatologist. There must be half-dozen dermatological syndromes named after him. Many countries invited him all over the world to speak and attend clinics to unravel mystery cases. To make a long story short, in 1955 he went to India where he lectured and attended a clinic where they lined up five cases for him. He evaluated the first four cases and came up with very unusual diagnosis, and his hosts were very grateful. The fifth case threw him for a loop. He studied the patient up and down. Finally, he realized he had no idea what he was looking at, so, as he tells it, he decided to invent some diagnosis. In his most professorial voice he said, "This is a very unusual case of multiple diffuse cutaneous erythematous maculopapulo vesiculo dissecans yada yada etcetera. At that, the audience laughed, and the smiling narrator said, "No doctor, this is a case of smallpox.

"I tell you this true story just to let you know that if an American world authority couldn't diagnose a case of smallpox, what the heck will we do if we are ever confronted with it. We've never seen a case. With our old immunization against the disease, it's been wiped out in this country and the whole world, so I'm putting up these pictures on the staff bulletin board so you'll all have a chance to study them and become familiar with what a full-blown case of smallpox looks like. You'll be able to see the great variation in the disease. Any questions?"

"What happened to the old-timer?" asked Amanda.

"Made it to ninety-nine. Sharp as a tack right up to the end."

"It should happen to us all," said Amanda.

"Amen," said Pollard "Okay, enough of that diversion. I'm supposed to review some history of smallpox, so let's start. One learns about the history of immunology that way."

Pollard passed out some papers to those in attendance. "Here's an outline of what we should know: First, we'll have to learn how to give smallpox vaccinations, and how to treat the damn disease. Don't ask me how since there is no effective therapy to stop the disease in its tracks. Most of our therapeutic efforts will be supportive and symptomatic. Second, we'll need to learn about isolation of patients. Plus we'll need to learn about infection control and isolation techniques. The goal is not to have any of these patients in the hospital because it would be impossible to prevent further outbreaks, not to mention the risk to all personnel. Smallpox is one of the most contagious diseases the world has ever known. Home care will be crucial here. We'll need to be able to detect the disease in the earliest possible stage, so we can isolate the infected patient as well as contacts.

"Why is the potential so deadly?" continues Pollard. "Because there is a high mortality rate in those who've never been vaccinated, and that's an awful lot of us since they stopped vaccinating many years ago. Also we are a highly mobile population today. I can catch the bug here in Chicago, get on an airplane and go to Los Angeles and infect ten people on the plane and 100 people as I travel around the city."

"I can't believe we'll ever see a case," said Amanda.

"We're at war you know, or do you? Terrorism is rearing its ugly head. In this type of war, anything's possible. Did you know that smallpox has already been used as a biological weapon?"

"No, when?"

"It's claimed that the British did it during the French and Indian Wars in the United States. They gave American Indians blankets used by smallpox patients. It worked. The blankets wiped out about fifty percent of some tribes. Others claim that the Indians did not get the blankets from the British. Who knows what the truth is after so much time has passed? Of course, that was in the days before Edward Jenner did his work. His invention of vaccination made it less likely smallpox would be so virulent today, but don't forget we have not vaccinated since 1977, when smallpox was eliminated as a disease. That means that many people are susceptible who never had the vaccination. Even those who had it fifty or more years ago may no longer have immunity. If they have a little immunity left, and if they get smallpox today, those people may get a milder form of the disease. Since they may be ambulatory, they could pass it on to others."

"So the threat only comes from terrorists who might get their hands on the few stores of smallpox virus here and in Russia?" asked Amanda.

"That's right," said Pollard. "If they can get it they'll use it."

"It's hard to believe," said Amanda shaking her head.

"Believe it. You and I have lived in times of peace, or so we thought. We've ignored the terrorist attacks since the seventies. But if you talk to some of the real old-timers, they're convinced that what we're going through today is a repeat of the nineteen thirties and forties when Hitler plunged the world into hell."

"I don't want to think about it," said Amanda.

"Sorry, but you've got to. It's my responsibility as chairman of the department to educate you and the entire staff. We're better off prepared than not."

CHAPTER 14

Anthrax:

Steve was right, Ben thought. The smallpox vaccination site on his thigh crusted over and that meant he was immune to any future outbreak of the disease. Soon the crust would fall off and leave a scar. He could always explain it as an old burn or some other type of injury, but who would see it on my upper thigh? Steve is one smart cookie, but for me it would remain as a remembrance of an experience.

Ben had settled into Northwestern University where he was sure he would do well. He had tested out of a considerable amount of undergraduate mathematics. This meant that he would be able to complete his full thirty-hour math requirement in less than two years, enabling him to get a jump on graduate school. He was working at McDonald's to earn some money. He decided that the discipline was good for him. It allowed him to better apportion his time so as not to neglect his schoolwork as he had done in high school.

But the real reason he was able to concentrate so well was the Imam. Ben now knew the power of concentration and the importance of goal orienting your life. When he thought of himself in the past, it was as if he was thinking of someone else who had died, and he was now reborn. He remembered with dread the intermittent sadness he had felt, and when the cloud had come, he had suffered from a complete lack of motivation. This had the effect of stopping all forward progress. He had not been able to concentrate and thus could not work. It had been a struggle not to succumb to the darkness that had engulfed him. The worst part was the feeling of hopelessness and isolation. He had had these bouts enough during his high school years, so that the isolation from his peers was a given. They knew when to avoid him, and soon it became a constant avoidance. If he had any favorite activities, it was during the cloud period, as he called it, that he would lose all interest in pursuing them with the exception of lifting weights. This would give him a high and helped him fight his symptoms. It would even help him overcome the fatigue and thoughts of suicide that, at times, had crept into his consciousness like a slow moving fog.

But now, with daily thoughts of the Imam's teachings, with focus on the goal, with lifting weights and above all with mathematics, he was reborn. He was important. He had a new mission. It felt good. He smiled as he thought of his future task as a holy warrior. He would show them a thing or two.

Then Ben would think of the other half of his past life, when he had experienced a sudden decreased need for sleep. It was at such times that he had developed a hostile attitude, and it had caused him trouble. He remembered striking the boy whom he had bumped into in the high school hallway. It felt as if he had shifted into high gear. He became angry and labile. Rage would occur for no apparent reason. The slightest stimuli could set him off. He became distractible and it became impossible to concentrate for longer than a minute or two. During these periods, he had experienced excessive energy and strength, and this was when he could lift heavier weights than he had been able to lift. Thank goodness these symptoms too are gone. He now knew how to control himself. He, or rather the Imam, had merged his various personalities into one. He knew that this oneness had to remain a oneness as long as he was involved with the Chicago holy war. He was on his own, for the Imam had given instructions that Ben was never to call him by phone, and never send letters or e-mails. All communication would now cease between Ben and the Imam. Ben would now work only with Steve until the Chicago project was over. Then Ben would receive further instructions in yet an unspecified manner and time. Ben wondered what his assignment would be, but he had a good idea, and he would be ready.

On Tuesday evening at 6:00 o'clock, Ben knocked on Steve's apartment door. "You're right on time, Ben. Let me see your smallpox scar."

Ben lowered his pants and showed Steve. "Perfect, Ben. It looks great. You'll never get smallpox when the others spread the good tidings to all of

Chicago's infidels. Congratulations. We're almost finished protecting you. I'll give you another anthrax immunization."

"Where do you get this stuff?" asked Ben.

"I'll give you the same answer I got when I asked the same question."

"What's that?"

"It's none of your business. As I think I mentioned once before, I am the only one you'll know in this whole operation. You'll never meet the other two involved, and they'll never meet each other, or you. If you don't know who you're working with you can't spill the beans as the infidels say. Get it, Ben?"

"Yes, I get it. A clever policy; it makes sense."

"Good, Ben. I like you. You're a fast learner. Now let me tell you what you'll be getting. There are certain things you should know. This vaccine, made from a certain strain of anthrax bacteria, does not have the power to cause the actual disease. It is not a live or dead vaccine. I mean it does not consist of live or dead bacteria. Either one can cause a person to develop immunity, you see. Because the vaccine doesn't contain whole bacteria, it's called an inactivated vaccine. This vaccine contains a protein called PA. That stands for protective antigen, and the PA comes from the anthrax bacteria. This PA helps your body make antibodies that fight and kill all the different strains of the anthrax germ."

"I get it," said Ben.

"Good."

"I've been reading, and I know that there are thousands of strains of anthrax bacteria," said Ben.

"That's right, Ben, and the PA in the vaccine makes antibodies that circulate in the blood stream and could kill whatever strain comes along, with one caveat."

"What's that?"

"This vaccine, like most vaccines, is not 100 percent perfect. It's considered protective for eighty percent of those who get it. So, in this case, when we introduce the anthrax to the infidels, we'll all take a certain antibiotic called Cipro, short for Ciprofloxin. The combination of the vaccine plus the Cipro should give us 100 percent protection. You'll start the medicine the day before we spread the germs and continue it for two months. Here are the pills. They're unlabeled. Hide them in a safe place where no one could find them. Keep a couple in your wallet at all times in case we have a change of plan and you have to take some early when you're not home. Understand?"

"Yes, Steve."

"Let's have your arm, Ben." Before Ben was ready, Steve had injected him. He felt nothing. "There, how's that, Ben? I'm getting pretty good at this. I'll see you one week from tonight. You'll have all your final instructions. Any questions?"

"None. I'm ready. God is Great. And you did say that I am not to participate with the others in this first phase of the process, right?"

"Right, Ben, we're saving you for the best."

Ben smiled because he believed he knew what his assignment would be.

CHAPTER 15

Detective Richard Galinski:

It was time for Amanda's bi monthly Friday evening visit to her parents for dinner. She arrived at her parent's home and her father greeted her.

"How are things going at work, Amanda?"

"Great, dad, I learn something new every day. I recently saw a case of chicken pox."

"Oh, poor kid," said her mother, Rose. I remember when you had your case. But I thought they give shots today so that kids don't get it anymore."

"They do. This wasn't a kid. This was a fifty some year old man, and he had chicken pox pneumonia, which is a serious condition. When adults get chicken pox it could be deadly."

"How'd he do?" asked her father.

"He made a good recovery," said Amanda. "It got Dr. Pollard talking about small pox, and he gave a lecture on it, because we have to be alert to the possibility of terrorist threats nowadays, and we have to have policies to address it."

"I know what you mean," said Amanda's father, Detective Richard Galinski. "The Chicago police department has to have plans in place also. In fact, the city of Chicago has worked on it, and we even had a drill to test the emergency planning of the city."

"How did it go, dad?"

"Not too well. They've stockpiled supplies to deal with smallpox and other bio threats, but once the supplies get on the scene there are no plans for distribution. The conclusion was that we need a lot more work to fine-tune the plan."

"I can't even begin to think what would happen if smallpox would come back. Many younger adults have never been vaccinated."

"Chaos is what would happen," said Richard. First, police and fire departments are short on staff all across the country. A lot of our guys that also serve in the military reserve are overseas, and that's true all over, so the departments are more understaffed than they were before 911."

"It's scary," said Rose.

"I agree," replied Richard. "I will say this though. The governor wanted all of us to be sure we all knew that the State of Illinois is one of only six states that got a green rating as far as preparation for bio-terrorism is concerned. Rose, hand me that briefcase on the buffet, please." Richard took out some papers and continued. "Amanda, it says here that Illinois has implemented the Illinois-National Electronic Disease Surveillance System, so that hospitals and doctors can electronically report infectious diseases, and be able to respond right away if any emergency pops up. And here there's a system for tracking two hundred Illinois hospitals on the web so they can see where there are beds available in case they're needed."

"What about the personnel? Where will they get the people?" asked Amanda.

"It says that there are twelve Illinois Emergency Medical Response Teams. They respond and assist whenever mass casualties occur. Each team is made up of a physician, nurse and paramedic that volunteer their time."

"I haven't been asked," said Amanda.

"Maybe they don't use residents," answered Richard.

"Anything else there in that report, dad?"

"Yeah, all the Illinois local health departments throughout the state are supposed to share resources in the event of emergency. There are ninety-five local health departments. Here's something else, too."

"What?"

"All hospitals are supposed to get chem packs to protect against nerve gas attacks. Did your hospital get one, Amanda?"

"I don't know. I'll have to check with Dr. Pollard. We're having meetings on the subject now."

"And last but not least, the State Weapons of Mass Destruction Team is made up of the Illinois State Police, the Secretary of State Police, The Illinois Department of Public Health, the Illinois Environmental

Protection Agency and the Illinois Emergency Management Agency. This team is supposed to respond to a bio or chemical attack. They determine the agent used and decide how to respond."

"It sounds like they have things well organized dad," said Amanda.

"Maybe on paper, Amanda, but in a mass attack I doubt it. From what we at the police department have been told, a bacterial or viral attack will kill plenty of people, but with vaccination for smallpox and good antibiotics for infections like anthrax and plague, the problem could be cut short assuming we have the supplies and the people to get the city protected fast enough."

"That's a big if, dad."

"Yeah, I know. The real danger though is with a nuclear attack. That might kill hundreds of thousands and may make the city a ghost town for years. It seems unthinkable, but the people who lecture us say it's not a matter of if, but when."

"A nuclear attack? No!"

"We're at war, Amanda. Do you think the kind of enemy we face now would hesitate to use nuclear weapons?"

"I just find it all unbelievable."

"I'll have to introduce you to Ahmad one of these days."

"Who's that, dad?"

"He's a Muslim member of the police force, and a great cop. His family has lived in the United States for three generations. He has his own ideas about the war on terrorism. Once you listen to him, you'll get a whole new outlook on the subject. I'll invite him over for dinner some Friday night. You'll come too."

"Thanks, dad."

CHAPTER 16

Afghanistan-Pakistan border:

Abdul Saidadov's work was unfinished. One more project was on the agenda. This one would set the stage for the rest of the holy war. It might perhaps wake up the sleeping giant, as opposed to opening up one eye after 911. Much of the USA still did not realize that they were on the defense against religious zealots who wanted to control the world. They did not realize because economic conditions made them forget. Saidadov knew that any new terrorist act against the United States might open the eyes of all the Americans, but that was okay, because there would now be a line in the sand.

"It's all set, Imam. The cargo is packed away in the center of one of the hundreds of textile containers ready for shipment to Miami."

"Separation of the parts is guaranteed, Abdul?"

"It is. It is impossible for the parts to come in contact with each other."

"How are you sure?"

"I was there myself. It was done to exact specifications."

"Good. We don't want anything to happen until we get Allah's gift to the United States. Is the identification set?"

"Yes. Our men on the docks have the number of the container. In the morning it will be lifted aboard ship."

"How about Miami?"

"The cargo will be in the right hands within hours after landing in Miami."

"How are you so sure?"

"I'm told arrangements have been made to pick up the package and then have it transported to Chicago where it'll be placed in a storage bin.

We'll assemble it when the time is ready. There are a lot of steps to this process, Imam."

"Yes, and Allah is guiding it every step of the way. We will not fail. When will the shipment arrive in Miami?" asked the Imam.

"In fifteen days. Four days later it will be in a storage bin in Chicago."

"And the person assigned to deliver it?"

"Being primed and made ready,"

"God is Great. The Great Satan will soon learn of the power of Allah."

CHAPTER 17

Terrorism methodology:

We'll review the emergency preparedness policy. That's a yearly requirement now," said Pollard. "We're going to be in the forefront of efforts to contain such attacks, and that includes all doctors and nurses and other Emergency Department personnel."

"Is it really possible for us to make a difference? My father was suggesting we're far from prepared," said Amanda.

"He's right, Amanda, but we'll do the best we can. As physicians we're considered first responders, and we will be in the front lines along with all trained paramedics, firefighters, and police."

Gail Cowen added, "I've already oriented all the nursing staff to the policy so that when we have our joint physician, nurse, ED staff meeting before the mock attack we'll be ready."

"That's good, Gail." Pollard reached for some papers on his desk and started handing them out. "We've all got to be knowledgeable about chemical and biological agents that can be used by terrorists, so here's a list of potential agents and bacteria and viruses that they may use against us. Look them over. It outlines all the signs and symptoms caused by the various terror agents. The quicker we can identify the problem and make a diagnosis, the quicker we can put measures in place to minimize the effects on others."

"We didn't have a word about any of this in medical school," said Amanda.

"You're right, Amanda. Not only that, but we have 35,000 emergency physicians on board in this country, and our continuing educational courses have yet to set up any consistent training. We better wake up."

"The same thing is true in the nurse education curricula," said Gail.

"I know. We hope to do something about that. I sit on the board of the American College of Emergency Physicians, and we've been lobbying the United States Congress to provide some money so that we could start to set up a real-time system for bacterial, chemical, and nuclear surveillance. We also have organized a Partnership for Community Safety with other first responders. We've got to get ready."

"How's that all going?" asked Amanda.

"Slow, too slow; I get the feeling people are working in a dream state. They know what has to be done, but can't believe its going to happen."

"Wasn't 911 enough to wake people up?" asked Gail.

"Sometimes I don't think so," answered Pollard. It's hard for me to believe that that attitude exists when these weapons of mass destruction can cause thousands, maybe millions of casualties."

"My father feels that it's nuclear terrorism that poses the biggest threat. We can treat those who get the bacteria, the chemicals could be contained and would dissipate, but the nuclear could kill hundreds of thousands."

"The first people exposed to bacteria or chemicals could all die before we wake up to what's going on. For sure he's right about the nuclear, because that has immediate and long term effects, plus there are two kinds of nuclear attacks, you know."

"Two kinds?" said Amanda.

"Too much medical school has kept you away from the newspapers, my dear lady. First, we can have a nuclear explosion caused by a fission bomb like the one at Hiroshima. I read about it and I took notes. Let me see, yes here it is. The first thing that happens with the explosion is that the sky lights up with a brilliant white light. At the center of the explosion, it is so hot that almost everything melts in a fraction of a second. There is a fireball that six miles away is brighter than one hundred of our suns. The fireball begins to spread outward and upward into a mushroom cloud. Everything flammable for miles around bursts into flames including your clothes. You get third degree flash burns. The heat produces an area of very high pressure. This pressure, wave called a shock wave, includes nuclear radiation that could penetrate twenty inches of concrete. The shock wave flattens everything close to ground zero, and, as it expands, hurricane-force winds rush into the vacuum that the expanding gas has left behind, and as it rushes in it sweeps up whatever debris there is such as glass, concrete, masonry and steel. Talk about hell! If you were close, you couldn't ask for a faster way to go. If the bomb detonates in a densely populated area, hundreds of thousands could die, and that could include us if it detonated within a mile or so. Don't forget the terrible radiation poisoning effects on the body if one survives the initial blast."

"You make it sound like anyone can build a bomb," said Amanda.

"Anyone willing to take some risks, and with enough hate or fear in their hearts could, Amanda, but let's go on to the second type of nuclear threat; that's the dirty bomb. Here the terrorists would use a non-nuclear explosive device packed with very radioactive substances that would contaminate an area as large as the explosive, not to mention the distance the radioactivity would travel on a windy day. Of course, the explosion itself would kill, but the radiation could cause quick death, or have lingering effects on the body from burns and radiation effects such as an increase in malignancies."

"There's no defense against anything like that?" asked Amanda.

"There has been for sixty years, and that's another country having the bomb. Mutual destruction capability has worked to keep nuclear bombs capped, but now with terrorists possibly getting hold of the bomb, and their believing that its use could pave the way to an Islamic world, there is no longer the mutual destruction defense. If they get it they will use it. It would be considered their duty."

"What's the world coming to?" asked a depressed Amanda.

"It's changed, and we've got to be ready. Let's get on to the next item on the agenda. We've discussed biological terrorism, and I've given you as list of potential agents, but you need to understand how they disseminate. If they were smart about wind conditions, they could disseminate the bugs for maximum effect. They could put the agents in explosives; either in aerial bombs or improvised explosive devices, known as IED's. You've read enough about those in the newspapers. They could even contaminate food and water. These agents are invisible, odorless and tasteless. You breathe it in or eat it and it got you. You'll be sick tomorrow or in a week or in a month and the bad news about that is you'll never know where you caught it. You might catch it in Chicago, then travel to Europe and get sick there. The whole world would shut down. Any questions?" asked Pollard.

They shook their heads.

"The last item on the agenda is the chemical agents. Here we've got a different story than with the biological agents. Now we could be talking swift death as little as five minutes for some. They fall in different categories. The first one is the blister agent like mustard gas and lewisite. Mustard gas has an odor, like bad mustard. It can cause bleeding internally and can cause severe skin burns about four to ten hours after exposure. It can also cause severe eye burning. Get enough of it and it could be fatal. The same is true of lewisite.

"Next are the nerve agents like VX, sarin, tabun and soman. These agents interfere with nerve transmission. They can either kill you quickly or give you upper respiratory like symptoms, slurred speech, difficulty breathing, coughing, hallucinations, headache, loss of bowel and bladder control, convulsions, coma and death.

"Then you've got the choking agents like chlorine gas and phosgene gas. Chlorine has a choking smell and inhalation of this gas could suffocate you. Phosgene smells like musty hay. Inhale it and it'll react with water in your lungs to form hydrochloric acid and carbon monoxide. It'll give you chronic lung damage or death.

"Cyanide will kill you in five minutes if you inhale it in a high enough concentration. The least it would cause is chronic lung damage. The symptoms of inhalation could include rapid respiratory rate, breathing difficulty, headache, cardiac irregularities, vomiting, unconsciousness, convulsions and respiratory failure."

"Plenty of homework," said Amanda.

"Do it. Review it every so often, concentrate on your work, and hope we never have need for the information."

CHAPTER 18

A night on the town:

"Ben, why don't you come with us?" said Alan Kanter, a twenty-one year old Northwestern University senior student.

Ben, deeply engrossed in a textbook, looked up and said, "What did you say?"

"I said put the damn book down and come with us."

"I have to study."

"Jeez, Ben, live a little."

"Where are you guys going?"

"Maloney's on Rush Street. We're going to get something to eat, have a few drinks, and who knows, maybe we'll get lucky."

"I'm not old enough to get drinks."

"You can always get a coke, you know. The question is Ben, are you old enough to get lucky?"

"I think I better stay here and do my homework."

"Holy shit. Listen to the little prick. Do you believe it? You're already setting the curve around here. You got all straight A's sewed up tight. They don't give high, middle and low A's you know. It's just A, man. How bad do you want to make the rest of us look?"

The two other young men in the study hall nodded in agreement.

Yeah, they're right, thought Ben. I can't forget the goal that I have to keep focused on first and foremost. This would be the perfect assimilation, Imam. Let's be one of the boys. Fourier analysis can wait. I know it anyhow. "Okay, let's go and live it up a little," said Ben as he closed his math book and got up from his chair.

"Now you're talking, Ben."

The four of them went to Alan's car parked outside of the dormitory. They drove down Lake Shore Drive toward the Loop and turned on Division Street to Rush Street. Luckily, they found a parking place on a nearby side street. It was only 5:30 and the usual crowd had not yet arrived.

They walked into Maloney's foyer. To the left of the foyer was the restaurant, and on the right was the bar. Both areas were rectangular in shape and the same size, about twenty by forty feet. The restaurant had tables seating two to eight. The bar portion had a long bar with bar stools extending the full length of the rectangle along one wall. Booths occupied the opposite wall, and there were tables between the bar and the booths. The walls, covered with pictures of old Chicago, provided the ambience for a popular watering hole and food stop for Chicago's younger and singles set.

Seated at a table for four, they all ordered a hamburger and a beer, except for Ben who ordered a coke. "Check out the chicks at that table in the corner over there," said Alan.

"They look a little old to me," said Ben.

"Maybe for a novice like you, Ben, but for men of the world like us, they're just about right. If you're not up to it Ben, don't worry. You just come along and see the master at work." Then while brushing his hair back, and with an air of extreme confidence, Alan said to the other two, "How about I take two, and you guys take one apiece?"

"Are you going to talk to them now?" asked Ben.

"No, Ben, professional operators like us don't act like that. I can see that you're a rank amateur when it comes to the ladies. That's crude. You don't interrupt them while they're eating. They'll go in the bar after they finish their food. Girls like to shoot the breeze over a few drinks for a while; then's when I make my move."

"But what if they just want to talk to each other?"

"They do, Ben, unless handsome dogs like us come along. Then it's every chick for herself. And after the hottest one latches on to me, the leftovers are for you guys to haggle about. Don't eat too fast. I want to time our leaving the restaurant to when they finish their food and go in the bar."

"If they go into the bar, said Ben.

"Nobody comes in here just to eat. Mark my words, they'll be in the bar as soon as they finish eating and pay their food bill."

"How do you know?" asked Ben

"Been here many times. I know the place well. That's the way it works. Say, Ben, I meant to ask you. We're all seniors and you're a freshman. How the hell did you get into senior math classes?"

"I tested out of most of undergraduate math."

Ben's three classmates stared at each other in amazement.

"Holy shit, did you guys hear that? Where the hell did you learn the stuff. They don't teach it in high school," said Alan.

"I learned it myself."

Alan and the other two shook their heads. "That is damn amazing. What do you say we name him after the world's greatest mathematician, Gauss," said Alan.

"Yeah, that's good. Okay, Gauss," said one of the other men at the table.

Alan Kanter was a resident of Wilmette, Illinois and he was in his last year as an undergraduate in engineering. He was six feet two inches tall with dark blonde hair and blue eyes. He was handsome, often compared in appearance to Brad Pitt. The comparison had gone to his head, thought Ben.

"Hold it," said Alan. "The ladies are leaving. Give Ben eight bucks apiece. Ben, pay the bill and come into the bar. I want to be sure we get a table next to them. Let's go, guys."

Ben paid the bill and when he entered the bar, he saw his friends seated at a table next to the girls. Just as Alan planned it, thought Ben.

"Ben, sit down. I ordered a coke for you." Alan then turned his attention to the next table. Now he had an opportunity for a close up look, and he liked what he saw. These were women in the twenties and thirties, and three of them weren't wearing wedding rings.

Alan leaned back in his chair and turned to the occupants of the next table. "Excuse me, ladies. May I ask if you're all from Chicago?"

The four women turned and looked at Alan. "Why do you ask?" said the one Alan had his eyes on.

"Well you see, it's just that you ladies have such a sophisticated, cosmopolitan appearance, I thought perhaps you may be visiting here from Europe, and if that was true we would be delighted to offer you some good old-fashioned Chicago hospitality and answer any questions you might have. Or even better yet, it would be our pleasure and honor to show you around the city."

The four women looked at each other, a faint smile crossing their features. "Well that's very nice and thoughtful of you," said the spokeswoman staring at Allen with a come-hither look.

An emboldened Alan continued. "My name is Alan Kanter. I'm from the engineering department at Northwestern University. And my friends here are Vernon Wallace and Bob Richards and the young one is Ben Gauss."

"Gauss?"

"Yes indeed. That's definitely right, ladies. He's descended from the famous mathematician."

"Uh huh."

"What are your names, ladies?"

"This is Alice Hampton, to her right is Megan Godfrey, and to her left is Phyllis Lewis. My name is Amanda Galinski."

"What do you ladies do?" asked Alan.

"My three friends are nurses. We work together," said Amanda.

"Oh, then you're a nurse too?" said Alan zeroing in on Amanda.

"No, I'm a physician," said Amanda.

Alan's eyebrows shot up. "We'll I'll be. That is an incredible coincidence. I was just thinking that I haven't been to a doctor in such a long time, I thought maybe I should be getting a complete physical examination," said Alan.

"Oh, I'm so sorry, but I couldn't do that," said Amanda.

"How come? You're a doctor, aren't you? That's what you said."

"Oh yes, I'm a doctor, but I don't practice pediatrics," said Amanda with a sorrowful look on her face.

With that, the three ladies, Vernon, and Bob almost spat out their drinks and erupted into uproarious laughter. All except Ben, who just sat there expressionless, gazing into space.

Alan stared at the ceiling, his mouth agape, his lower lip drawn in. Then he turned his head down and looked at Amanda. He smiled, nodded his head and said, "That was a good one, lady. Are you sure you're not a stand up comic?"

"Nope, definitely not, Alan. Are you sure you're not one?" Then wide eyed Amanda, smiling, stared at Alan and said, "Well boys, it has indeed been a pleasure meeting you charming gentlemen, but if you don't mind we've got some very important things to talk about."

"Okay, I get the hint. It has been a pleasure meeting you charming ladies as well. Let's go guys." The men pulled out their wallets and left the bill and payment on the table. When Ben opened his wallet, three pills rolled out. What are those?" said Alan.

"Uh, what?"

"Those pills there?"

Ben looked down at the table. He quickly grabbed the pills and put them back in his wallet. "Just some cold pills," he said.

Amanda heard what Allen and Ben said, and she saw the pills. Those are Cipros, she thought. Why is he lying to his friends?

The boys left. Vernon Wallace started laughing again. "What the hell's so funny?" asked Kanter. Ben, looked at Vern.

"That lady doctor. What was her name? Amanda Galinski. Man, that was the best one-liner I ever heard," said Vern.

"Ha-ha, very funny. Shut up, Vern," said Alan.

CHAPTER 19

The last two Trojan Horses, Joe and Jenny:

Steve returned from work earlier than usual. He took off his suit, dressed into his casual clothes, grabbed his gym bag and headed for North Side Athletic Club. He would get a good workout, meet a few buddies and transact some important business. The club was only two miles away, but the Chicago traffic, at this time of day, made the trip a twenty-minute ride.

North Side was the oldest and busiest club in the city. Steve walked up the steps to get to the second floor main entrance. He signed in at the front desk and then entered the locker rooms adjacent to the sign-in desk. The weight rooms and all the exercise machines lined up almost as far as the eye could see were located on this level. The gym was on a lower level. One had to walk down the stairs to get to the gym and shoot some hoops unless there was a basketball or volleyball tournament in play. Also on this level were the racquetball and handball courts filled with well conditioned athletic and tournament caliber players. Surrounding the basketball court was a circular, eight laps to the mile, banked running track.

Steve walked two fast laps and ran fourteen more laps. Then he went upstairs to use the exercise machines. He started with the apparatus for upper body strength. Turning to the man in the adjacent machine he said, "What's new, Joe?"

Without so much as turning to Steve, and between exhalations, short, bald, pudgy Joe said, "Nothing, Steve."

"My car works like a charm since you got through with it," said Joe

"It was a piece of cake."

"Not to me it wasn't. The car was as dead as a doornail, as thy say. I still remember how you answered me when I asked how you find out what's wrong with a dead car."

"What did I say? I don't remember."

"You said, "I just screw around.""

"That's right. That's what I do. I just screw around until I find out what's wrong."

"Yeah, but I wouldn't even know where to start screwing," laughed Steve.

"That's because you're too intelligent to be smart," said Joe.

"Shit, Joe. I know what's on the dashboard, but I have no clue what's behind it."

"Yeah, but what the hell do I know about architecture?" said Joe.

"I get the point. Anything else new, Joe?"

"Not a thing."

Steve paused for a moment, grunted with the pull of the machine and said, "It's a go a week from Thursday. That's final. This is the last you'll hear from me."

"Okay. I'm looking forward to it."

"You remember what to do?"

"It's etched in my brain."

"You got your territory in mind?"

"Exactly."

"See you again, Joe."

"Bye Steve."

Steve went back to his grunting, and was soon ready to exercise his lower extremities. He went across the room to a different set of machines. Why not this one? There was a good-looking lady working out on the next machine. She was tall with pitch-black hair that hung shoulder length. She had full lips adorned with shiny red lipstick. She had thin eyebrows perfectly curved above large, bright hazel eyes. Both hands gripped the machine handles, and sparkling on the ring finger of each hand there was a beautiful golden ring with a large gemstone. She wore a tight black leotard that showed her lean curves in all their glory. Watching her work the leg machines was the epitome of sensuality.

"You're new here, aren't you?" asked Steve.

"Yes, I am," she answered without turning her head.

"Did you just join?"

"No. I'm getting a one day free trial to see if I like it."

"Oh, you'll like it all right. I've been here a year. I come three times a week. The only problem is that it stays crowded no matter what time of the day or night you come."

"Sounds like a good way to meet nice people."

"That's true, but I wouldn't be able to guarantee they're all nice. I can tell you this though, they're all pretty fit and healthy."

"As I look around here I can see that."

"What's your name?" asked Steve.

"Jenny. And what's yours?"

"Steve."

"What do you do, Jenny?"

"I'm in the retail business. I work in jewelry. How about you, Steve?"

"I'm an architect."

"How interesting."

"It's all set. A week from Thursday night, Jenny. The time has come to put the plan in place. Be ready."

Jenny nodded and smiled. "Uh huh."

"Are you ready?"

"I am ready and waiting and eager to start."

"Uh huh."

"You have your territory?"

"Definitely do, Steve, and I can't wait to go to work."

"Do you like the leg machines, Jenny?"

"They're a little harder than I thought."

"Don't overdo it. You might get sore muscles and hamper your work. You could set the tension a little lower you know."

"This is perfect, Steve. I need to build up my leg strength for all the walking I'll be doing when I present the infidels their gifts."

"Good talking to you, Jenny. Got to go now."

"Have a good day, Steve."

CHAPTER 20

Ben and a clinical diversion:

After the boys left Maloney's, the girls chuckled. "Amanda, that was brilliant. You cracked me up. You sure are quick with the one line joke," said Phyllis.

"I don't know how I thought of it. It just popped into my head," said Amanda.

"The guy was a good sport about it at least."

"That's true, he was that."

"On the other hand, those guys were pretty cute," said Alice.

"Gauss looked young enough to be my son," said Phyllis.

"Gauss? That's pretty funny. They must have nicknamed him that because he's probably the dorm's resident math genius," said Amanda.

"Serious looking little guy, wasn't he?" said Megan.

"Yeah, he was that. Those pills that dropped out of his wallet were Cipros. I'm sure they were. Gauss told his friends they were cold pills. Did any of you see the pills?" asked Amanda

They all shook their heads no. Alice said, "Maybe he's being treated for a urinary tract infection."

"That's a possibility," said Amanda. "It's kind of rare in young men though. Oh well, it's none of our business. Let's talk about the PI Committee. That's what I got us together for. I need to learn all I can."

PI, or Performance Improvement, is a hospital-wide activity involving all members of the health care team working in a collaborative way to improve care and promote safety for all hospital patients. Pollard had assigned Amanda to the Emergency Medicine Department Performance Improvement Committee, and she decided that inviting the three veteran nurse members of the committee to dinner and drinks would be a good way to get oriented to its function.

The next morning Amanda arrived in the Emergency Department the same time as an ambulance carrying an elderly patient who was semiconscious, confused, and disoriented. He was an eighty-four year old man, a resident of the Lakeside Assisted Living Center. His wife, also a resident, was available to give a history. A medical report from the center accompanied the patient. Amanda read the report. The patient was not capable of giving a medical history. Amanda introduced herself to the wife.

"What happened to your husband, Ms. Coletti?"

The animated, gray haired and rotund Ms. Coletti, with arms and hands punctuating her words said, "Oh I'm so worried. He was okay until yesterday. I knew something was wrong because he didn't want to get out of bed. When I asked him he said he felt weak and wanted to sleep some more. He doesn't really sleep too good because he's always getting up to go to the bathroom at night. Anyhow, when he waked up he seemed a little confused. He sat in the chair and had a little something to eat, but not much. He just picked at the food. That's the way he was most of the day. The nurse checked him and said he didn't have any fever, and his blood pressure and pulse were okay. He went to sleep early, but when he woke up at about five in the morning, he was delirious. He was breathing fast. He didn't know me, and now he for sure had a fever. I felt him and he was hot. The nurse checked him and said his belly was tender and his temperature was 102, so she called the doctor and then she got the ambulance, and here we are."

"Does he have any allergies to any medicines, Ms. Colletti?"

"No, doctor."

Amanda continued taking a recent and past medical history while at the same time examining the patient. She found his heart rate to be 130 and regular. Blood pressure was 96 over 50. "Does he have a history of heart trouble, Ms. Coletti?"

"No, not that I know of."

She listened to his lungs and heard the characteristic cellophane like crackling that is usually consistent with either pneumonia or congestive heart failure. She did not see any cardiac medications on the record from the assisted living center. As soon as she examined the patient's abdomen, she identified the potential source of the problem. The urinary bladder was palpable almost to the level of the umbilicus. He had a distended bladder, and he winced with discomfort when Amanda palpated the area. Rectal examination revealed an enlarged prostate with no palpable nodules consistent with a diagnosis of benign prostatic hyperplasia, although the possibility of prostatic carcinoma was also under consideration. Amanda felt that the patient had a urinary tract infection from the distended bladder, causing a breeding ground for bacteria. This was critical. Fast action is necessary to reverse the process, or the patient would die of sepsis (blood poisoning). I hope it isn't too late thought Amanda.

"Phyllis take some orders, please."

"Yes, doctor."

"These are stats. Insert a Foley catheter and get a urine culture. Drain slowly—he's got severe bladder distention. Record input and output and get a stat cbc, electrolytes, bun and creatinine, blood culture times two, ecg and portable chest AP. Start IV 5% Dextrose in half-strength saline. Got it all? Read it back, please."

"Yes doctor."

"Good, Phyllis. As soon as the IV's going, and we have the blood and urine cultures, we'll start antibiotics."

Ms. Coletti, still present in the room, asked, "Is he bad, doctor?"

"It is serious, Ms. Coletti. It looks like he developed a severe urinary tract infection. He's got a paralyzed bladder, and the infection is spreading into his blood stream. We'll put him on antibiotics, and drain his bladder and have him watched in Intensive Care."

With both fists covering her mouth, Ms. Coletti nodded her head.

Amanda tried to comfort her. "We'll start therapy now. Who is Mr. Coletti's doctor, ma'am?"

"Dr. Hayes," she answered without hesitation.

"We'll get hold of him and bring him up to date."

"Does he have a chance, doctor?"

"He does, Ms. Coletti. His condition is serious, but he has a decent chance."

Amanda spent a busy day working and seeing a wide variety of patients ranging in age from two months to Mr. Coletti's eighty-four years. After she finished she made a brief stop in Intensive Care and noted with satisfaction that Coletti's temperature improved, and his blood pressure was now 118 over 68. Maybe we got him in time, she thought. It was a Friday night and she headed for her parent's home for dinner. This was the dinner where her father was to invite Ahmed for a discussion on the terrorism threat.

CHAPTER 21

Ahmed:

Ahmed was a forty-two year old with a full head of straight black hair. He was medium height and dressed in slacks and sport jacket over a white shirt without a tie. When he met Amanda, he bowed and took her hand.

"I heard so much about you," he said.

Amanda was impressed with his polite demeanor. He had a closed mouth smile and spoke a little above a whisper. During dinner the conversation mostly centered on small talk with Amanda explaining some of the details of her work. Then they had dessert and coffee and Richard said, "Ahmad, my daughter could use the kind of education you've been giving us at the police department."

"My pleasure," said Ahmad. He turned to Amanda, and spoke in a very calm voice. "Very few people I speak to have a real understanding about the threat facing the free world. What do you think, Amanda?"

"I find it all like a bad dream. I keep thinking it will just go away."

"That would be great, wouldn't it? But it's not going to happen. When do you think it all started?" asked Ahmad.

Amanda reflected for a moment before she answered. "As far as I was concerned, and I recognize now that there was a lot of unawareness on my part, and my answer would e be September 11, 2001, but others tell me it has been going on since the seventies."

"That's true, Amanda. They have slowly targeted America. First of all, you have to understand something about Islam. The word itself means submission. A Muslim is one who believes in the word of Allah, and is obedient to that word. According to the Prophet of Islam, Allah wrote the Koran. A Muslim has to do just as the book says. If one does not, then he or she is not a Muslim. It's as simple as that. Many Muslims would never consider me a member of the faith. As far as Islamic scholars are concerned, the Holy Book will remain unchanged throughout eternity; because every word is the word of Allah and every word is law. Every Muslim I know wants peace, and that represents the very great majority, but Islamic zealots, the people who we are fighting against, have their own interpretation. These zealots are certain that they are the only true Islamic faith…"

Amanda interrupted, "But these people are such a small minority, how can they achieve their will?"

"Through fear, through armed might, through an ideology that allows no dissent. What would you do, Amanda, if you were an average citizen with children living in a rural area, who suddenly found their community overrun with many armed people? Would you fight? Are you armed? Just think of Iran, a country controlled by zealots. The majority of their young people would prefer a more democratic regime, but they're helpless to do anything about it. Fear is a powerful force, and it is powerful enough to cause people to sit by and watch as others take over. Zealots believe that if they die for Allah they are guaranteed life after death, and all the rewards that go with paradise. They believe that Christians make no sense with their Trinity. It will doom them to hell. That's an example of how the zealots think. Jews, of course, are no different. They are trespassers on Muslim lands and must leave one way or the other unless they bow to Islamic thinking."

"What are you suggesting that this country do?" asked Amanda.

"In my opinion the greatest threat facing not only the United States, but the entire free world, is ignorance about the fact that all Islamist fanatical groups like Al-Qaeda and Isis and others want to control the world. I don't know when we'll wake up. Another attack might do it, and even after that, you'll still have people saying we should abolish our army. The avowed goal of groups like those that I mentioned is to take over the Middle East and establish an Islamic Empire there. Then the rest of the world should follow. Maybe it'll take 100 years, but so what. They can wait. They are very patient, and that is their best weapon."

"I once saw Osama Bin Laden on TV years back. He offered a truce. Is that even a possibility?" asked Amanda.

"They define truce as time to regroup, time to refresh and time to rearm so as to prepare for the next attack. They offer a truce before they attack. That's to hope you'll lower your defenses. That's all it means."

"You offer a hard line."

"Still not as hard as theirs. Do you find all this hard to believe, Amanda?"

"I surely do. It's inconceivable to me. I know it's all there, but I just can't seem to be able to deal with it."

"Well then, let me quote a captured Al-Qaeda document. I've committed it to memory: 'Al-Qaeda is committed to a Holy War against dictators of the earth and secular groups that will end only when everyone believes in Allah.'"

"Just talk, that's all it is."

"What do you think would have happened if we lost World War II, Amanda?"

"Maybe we'd be speaking German or Japanese."

"Well, that's sort of a light hearted answer, but I get your meaning. We'd be living under Fascism. If we were Jewish we'd be dead. That's one of the things that would happen. You need to understand that we could lose this war, and I know you find that hard to believe, as do most people. The reason is that none of you conceive that what's happening now is a World War."

Amanda shook her head.

"And it's not the usual World War as we're used to thinking about wars," said Ahmed

"What do you mean?"

"We think about wars in terms of large armies capturing territories, marching and fighting until one country is defeated, and then the war is over. As far as we're concerned now, in relation to what's happening with terrorism, we conceive of this war as a war on terror, so we fight against a tactic used by the enemy. This tactic isn't new. We don't have a chance of winning if this is our mindset. We must think of this struggle in terms of the fact that we are fighting against a unified philosophy, and this philosophy has its sights on the institution of Muslim law over a completely unified Islamic world. If we concentrate on fighting terror, and lose sight of their goal, then we can't possibly win. How do we win if we fail to identify the enemy?"

"The enemy is men who lead groups like Al-Qaeda, and Isis and other groups whose names I don't even know anymore, answered Amanda."

"Then you might as well surrender now and save needless slaughter," said Ahmad.

"I don't understand," said Amanda.

"How do you feel about religion, Amanda?"

"Personally?"

"No. In general."

"Well, in general I believe that one should practice whatever religion they embrace, and that we should respect each other's beliefs."

"That's good, and that's just what we want in this country."

"Okay, so?"

Ahmed took a deep breath and a drink and said, "Men like Osama Bin Laden in the past and al-Baghdadi of Isis and others want only one religion on this earth. That's their goal, and they will use terror to achieve it. They feel that is their religious necessity"

"They've made that clear to the world, didn't they," said Amanda.

"Yes, they did," said Ahmed. "What's happened here in the United States? We had some solidarity after 911. It's gone now. Is this a surprise? It hardly is when the greatest power on earth is facing tough economic times. We have the right and the left hating each other. Two armed camps, and it's getting worse. I forget who it was who said, 'a nation divided amongst itself can not stand.' Well, in this case, when we are facing such a unified force against us, as we stay divided, and exude weakness we are easy prey to our enemies."

"I have two questions, Ahmad. If you feel so strongly that our division in this country will cause our defeat, then how do we change? How do we unify?"

"The best answer I can give you, Amanda is that it will probably take a series of tragedies for us, and those tragedies, which I'm certain are coming, may unify us through a gradual education process. Our low solidarity at this time is our greatest danger. I'm afraid change will be slow. What's the other question?"

"How do we change our enemies to think differently?" asked Amanda.

Ahmed nodded his head and said, "The only thing I can think to do is to show them that radical Islam is a failed philosophy. We did it for Fascism in 1945. We did it for Communism in the 1980s. We did that through a show of commitment and strength, and we have to do it again. While we do this, we have to help the moderate Muslims believe that there is another option; that religious freedom is not such a bad idea, that they must speak against and oppose the terrorist element in their religion.

"Zealots have a tendency to put in writing what they plan to do long before they do it. I remind you of Osama's quote. The zealot before WWII was Adolf Hitler. He laid out his plans in *Mein Kampf,* which translated means My Struggle. Most people didn't take him seriously, but Churchill said Hitler was crazy and dangerous. Churchill was right. Hitler carried his plans out sixteen years later. We have to believe the present day zealots like Isis, Al-Qaeda and the Iranian Ayatollah, all screaming for the destruction of the little Satan, Israel and the big Satan, the United States. We have to believe what they say, for their convictions are inbred from birth."

With that comment, Richard shook his head and rotated two antique marbles in his right hand; marbles which were the clue that led to finding the murderer in his first case as a detective and used as a calming mechanism when deep in thought ever since.

CHAPTER 22

Hamas and Jami Alemadi:

The goal has always been to destroy Israel; and for the Hamas movement, Palestine is the central location for the development of Islamic political power where the establishment of a head of a Muslim state will trigger reawakening in the Islamic world. This for one purpose alone—Holy War.

Hamas considers the territory of present day Israel, as well as the Gaza Strip and the West Bank as a religious bequest from Allah, and these territories can never be under the domination of non-Muslims. They also believe that all Muslims have a religious duty to join the struggle to wrest control of the land from Israel. Simply stated, resolution of the Arab-Israeli conflict requires the destruction of the Jewish state. There is no compromise with this statement.

The thirty-six articles of the Hamas Covenant details the primacy of Islam in all aspects of life. The Hamas slogan is "God is its target, the Prophet is its model, the Koran is its constitution, Holy War is its path and death for the sake of Allah is the loftiest of its wishes."

Jami Alamadi grew up in Gaza. Her father was a prominent member of the Hamas organization. As is usually the case, he had powerful enemies. He suffered a mysterious death by gunshot. The killer was never apprehended, but it was easy to assume that Israel's Mossad, or the Israel Defense Force was responsible (although they denied all responsibility), and that's where the issue was left. Jami's father, as with all politicians, had some vocal political opponents, but Hamas authorities did not question them.

Jami was thirteen years of age at the time of her father's murder. After his death, she was inconsolable. She had loved her father who had inculcated her with the Hamas philosophy, and she vowed to continue her father's work. Her mother sent her to relatives in London where she completed high school. She attended a radical Islamist mosque where she heard the words that reminded her of her father. This only strengthened the hatred she felt for Israel. She learned that she could do more by residing in the United States where she could assist Hamas and turn her attention to the Great Satan, the protector of Israel.

By 1990, Hamas had developed a sophisticated presence in the United States. One of the first places Jami (now known as Jenny Alberts) went to was Chicago. Here, in one of the Mosques of the city, she and twenty other members learned about the use of explosives and their placement in cars. The purpose was to receive training to return home and utilize their newfound talent against Israel. Jenny, however, would have none of that suggestion, insisting that she would stay in the United States, where she knew that the holy war would make itself felt in time. Hamas agreed when she proved her worth in an unusual way. It turned out that there was an American infiltrator in their midst who was a member of the Federal Bureau of Investigation. Jenny asked for one month to resolve the problem. She struck up a personal friendship with the infiltrator that blossomed into a relationship that within three weeks ended in her bed. She then called for her associates from the mosque. When they arrived at her apartment they found the FBI infiltrator naked, face down in bed, a bullet in his right temple, and a knife in his left upper posterior chest. The FBI man disappeared. A plaque in a corridor of FBI headquarters honoring lost heroes that had worked for the organization and were missing—or killed in action—commemorated this lost hero. For this act, Hamas honored Jenny who became a United States citizen and raised much money for Hamas.

When word of her exploits reached the ears of the Imam, he had Steve contact her and offer her a place on his team. She was initially skeptical, but he assured her that as a team member she would be involved in a devastating attack against the Great Satan that would make all previous attacks from the seventies on, including 911, pale into insignificance. Even though Steve would not give her full details at that time, she sensed his sincerity and agreed. She was the quintessential Trojan Horse.

CHAPTER 23

Jamal Abu Hadid:

Jamal Abu Hadid was born in Saudi Arabia in 1976. His father was a wealthy businessman who was on a first name basis with the royal family. Like most Saudi Arabians, they practiced an austere form of Islam that literally interprets the Koran. Known as Wahhabism, it began to flourish in the 1970's when Saudi Arabian charitable organizations began funding Wahhabi religious schools.

Jamal Abu Hadid learned from age seven on that Wahhabis are the chosen ones who will see paradise. The rest are Christians, Jews, and even Muslims who do not share the Wahhabi faith. Jamal learned that it was his duty to fight and kill Jews, and he took the message to heart.

The Wahabbi movement is committed to the establishment of Muslim states based only on Islamic law. Besides Saudi Arabia, Wahabbis reside in every other Muslim country. Most do not have militias. Some, like the Taliban, who believe in Wahhabi principles, do have a militia. Bin Laden was a Wahhabi. The great majority of suicide bombers are Wahhabis.

Jamal took to his religious training and at his father's insistence he attended college at the University of Illinois in Chicago where he received a degree in mechanical engineering. The entire time he studied at the University he also attended religious services at a mosque where he fell under the influence of a radical cleric who continued to imbue him with Wahhabism. When he graduated with his degree, it was expected that he would return to Saudi Arabia, but he made a conscious choice to stay in the United States where he would merge and become a fighter for Allah; another perfect Trojan Horse. He changed his name to Joe Harris, became an American citizen, and started working in a small engineering firm based out of Chicago. His family back home had no idea about their son's radical mindset.

Joe was a mechanical genius and he devoted this talent to the development of sophisticated bombs capable of detonation in all manners of electronic and mechanical wizardry. He attended a Chicago area explosive school located in the western suburbs. Here, like-minded men and women came to learn how to build these weapons. They took the knowledge back to Palestine and other areas of the world to join the struggle against the Great Satan and her allies.

The Imam praised Joe's work as the type of expertise necessary to implement the Chicago Holy War. The Imam told Steve. Steve approached Joe and he eagerly came on board anxious to strike a blow for his faith.

CHAPTER 24

Terrorism methodology:

Ben knew the time was fast approaching. He would see Steve tomorrow night for final instructions. Perhaps it was anxiety over the coming meeting, but whatever it was, Ben noted that the cloud had returned. Ben found himself struggling over one of the extra credit math problems. He could not solve it, and the more he tried the more he felt the cloud returning. This was a new experience. He had never had to ask for help before, and he wasn't going to now. This was a problem in the vector calculus, a subject easy for Ben, so why was he having so much trouble? With the solution of the problem, the cloud would dissipate. Ben knew this, and continued to work. He started from the beginning, checking each step in the process, but his answer remained different from the one in the textbook. The answer of infinity in the textbook made no sense. Finally, Ben concluded that he was right and the book was wrong. He had never seen an answer like infinity. He would tell his professor the next time he had class. This thought stabilized the cloud for the time, enabling Ben to sleep. He had an important job to do. He was not yet told what the job was, but he was almost positive he knew, and it would demand his complete attention—there was much at stake

The next day was Tuesday and Ben had a full day of classes. His last class ended at four o'clock, so this would give him plenty of time to arrive at Steve's apartment by 6:00. He might even have some time to run a fast check on the math problem. He rushed to his dormitory from class and sat down to his dilemma. He again arrived at the same answer, further reinforcing his conviction that the answer in the book was absurd. The more he fell into this dilemma, the more his conviction about his new mission with Steve began to falter. Was this disrupting my mission, he thought?

Nevertheless this would be a big day in his life. He would not be taking part in the start of the Chicago Holy War, but there was still his unknown mission he hoped to soon learn about. He smiled. He knew there were others involved in this first phase, and he was pleased that he would never know who the other participants were, except for Steve. He knocked on Steve's front door exactly at 6:00. Steve opened the door. "Come in, Ben."

Steve was surprised at Ben's appearance. "Are you okay, Ben? You look upset. Are you worried about something?"

"I've been working on a math problem. It's got me stumped, or the book answer is wrong. I'm not sure which."

"You need a clear mind for what we and you are soon about to do."

"I know. I know. I have to focus. I can. I have to. I know the courses and the subjects get harder and the problems get tougher."

"Remember Ben, We struggle to acquire the knowledge of Allah while we are here on earth. That is our task. Someone, I can't remember who, said 'God is a mathematician.' He has all the secrets of the universe in his mind, and when we arrive in paradise, the secrets will become clear to us. We will have the mind of Allah. There will not be any unsolvable problems. There will be no worry. There will be no anxiety or depression. There will be only peace. You will never again have a problem with math, because the mind of Allah will be your mind, granted for all eternity to those of us who fight Allah's Holy War. We are fortunate to be part of a doctrine that guarantees so much for true believers."

Ben eyes opened wider. "Yes, I know Steve. I feel that with all my heart." Steve looked at Ben. His facial expression was still not serene. He had a special task for Ben after the ones he would discuss tonight, and Ben needed to be primed and ready.

"Do you have the pills I gave you, Ben?"

"Yes. I have three of them in my wallet, and the rest of them are hidden in my room at the dorm."

"Good, Steve. They will protect you. You will start taking the pills tonight. Ben, We need you for the last phase of our project...the most important phase."

Ben's heart beat faster. That was it. This meant that they would soon start the Holy War.

Steve walked into the kitchen and drew a glass of water. "Take one pill now with this water. Then you will take one pill every twelve hours for the next two months. You have to take it twice a day."

"I will."

"You will be protected for certain. You will be free to work."

"Just tell me what to do, Steve."

They were sitting at the dining room table, and Steve reached over to the buffet, retrieved two boxes, and gave them to Ben. "These are what your associates will be using in our first phase, Ben."

Ben looked at the boxes. One was a square cube with sides about sixteen inches. The second was a rectangular box about twelve by five inches. The larger box was much heavier than the smaller one. The boxes were made of ordinary layers of cardboard.

"There are two smaller and tougher inner boxes within the cardboard boxes. Thursday is when we'll start disseminating the infidel's gifts. Have you ever used a breath spray, Ben?"

"No."

"But you've seen people using them, haven't you?"

"Oh yes, I've seen them used."

"One can hold these sprays in their hand and that will hide them. They won't do much to freshen one's breathe, Ben, but they will stop the breath of the infidels though, because they contain aerosolized smallpox." Your associates know what to do, Ben."

"I see," said Ben.

"They can be held in one's hand and you can pretend that you're using them as a breath spray. You can spray them anywhere and no one will know it. The secret is just to act normal. If one sprays these along airport ticket lines, they'll take the virus to other parts of the country. Everyone infected could easily infect ten others.

"I got it, Steve. What's in the other box?" asked Ben.

"There you have your anthrax, Ben. Only these are not aerosol cans. There are twenty-one small envelopes in the box. The envelopes are as small as the aerosol cans, but they are triple ply, and they contain a white powder, so fine that you can't see it once it is spread around. What you have in these envelopes is highly weaponized anthrax. Any unvaccinated person and person not taking Cipro who breathes it in will be in serious trouble. So you see, Ben, the infidels will be presented with a double whammy at the same time. Each of your associates has a week supply of both weapons. The infidels won't know what hit them. Can you imagine the chaos when people start coming down with both of them? Smallpox will be the first disease to show up. We're going to have a lot of doctors screwing up diagnosis all over the place. It's going to be fun to watch the news, Ben. We'll know what's going to happen before anyone else." Steve clapped his hands and laughed aloud. "God is great," laughed Steve. "That he is," answered Ben.

CHAPTER 25

More Trojan Horse territories:

The next day Steve drove from work directly to Northside Athletic Club. Instead of driving his car, he drove a Toyota SLE minivan with mid and back seats removed. He loaded two suitcases in the back. He had one appointment at 6:00, and one at 7:00. He arrived at the club by 5:15, put on his gear and went down to the track. After all the intense planning for the last year, the time had come, and he was surprised at how calm and relaxed he felt. His warm-up was vigorous this evening, and his run also included intermittent sprints around the banked track. He spent thirty minutes running, and then took a quick shower.

At 6:00, he met Joe who was working out on the same machines he had worked on before. He walked by Joe and told him he would meet him in the bar in a few minutes. He ordered two cokes, sat down at one of the tables, and waited.

Joe lived on the south side of Chicago, in an area known as Hyde Park. He and Steve discussed the locations where Joe would disseminate the smallpox and anthrax. He would concentrate his activities around the University of Chicago, the Museum of Science and Industry and a number of shopping centers as far south as Calumet City. Then they went to their respective cars, and Steve gave Joe the smaller box containing the anthrax envelopes. Since Joe had perfected the smallpox aerosols, he already had his supply. Joe listened to the same instructions as Ben, including the start day of Thursday. Then with a mutual God Is Great, they parted company.

Steve went back into the club and went to the leg machines. He worked out for about ten minutes until 7:00. Promptly at that time, Jenny arrived. This time she had on a tight, red T-shirt and shorts, which matched her lipstick. They worked out on the machines for about fifteen minutes and then went to the bar where they spoke. Jenny received her instructions. She lived in the center of the city in a condominium not far from the University of Illinois Chicago campus, a few miles southwest of the Loop. Steve assigned her to this main downtown section filled with shops, theaters, the Field Museum, the Shedd Aquarium and the Adler Planetarium, locations filled with locals and tourists. She received full instructions about the handling of her twin weapons.

"Don't dress so flashy, Jenny. Try not to look so beautiful. You don't want any attention drawn to yourself."

"Blimey, Steve, you sure know how to flatter a gal. Don't worry. I'll be just a plain old, no make-up, Jane."

They left the club and walked to the parking lot. Steve transferred two boxes to Jenny's car trunk.

Steve's assignment was to concentrate on Michigan Avenue's 'magnificent mile,' one of the most expensive miles of real estate in the world, filled with expensive shops. He would also spend time at Navy Pier with its Imax Theater, parks, gardens, restaurants and attractions. He would have to start his activities next week rather than Thursday, because this evening he set out for Florida, figuring he would drive about four hours, stop at a motel and arrive at his destination tomorrow.

CHAPTER 26

Alama Aziz:

Alama Aziz received his Ph.D. in physics from the University of Zurich in 1982. He went back to his native Pakistan and worked in the nuclear program. He was religious, quiet and intense, once quoted as saying that "All western nations are not only enemies of Pakistan, but are enemies of Islam." He believed that "the nuclear bomb was necessary to protect Islam from the enemies of Islam." He began to keep the company of like-minded scientists and non-scientists. In 1995 he left his work and joined the Holy Warriors in Afghanistan where he fought for two years. He met Osama Bin Laden who recognized his worth and sent him back to Pakistan where he would "prove to be a valuable resource for the global Holy War." He worked there until 1999, and then he disappeared. At the same time, highly enriched uranium also disappeared. The Pakistan government preferred to keep this information from the world community.

Stolen nuclear material is a real concern for the world, and now with terrorism raising its ugly head the main target is the United States. If the terrorists were to design a ten-kiloton nuclear weapon, and exploded it in a large city, there would result a circle of near-total destruction that would be two miles in diameter.

Alama Aziz stated that the acquiring of weapons of mass destruction is a "religious duty." Crude nuclear bomb design drawings were found in Al-Qaeda camps in Afghanistan. The only ingredient necessary is highly enriched uranium (HEU), and terrorists could easily make a gun type bomb by firing one mass of HEU into another mass. The bomb might be smuggled across the United States border intact, or brought across our border in pieces and assembled here.

Aziz disappeared and no one knew where Aziz went, but Aziz was busy, and he worked on fashioning a nuclear device. It was similar to the "Little Boy" nuclear bomb of Hiroshima fame in 1945. He decided to use a bomb shaped cylinder. On one end of the cylinder, he placed a sub-critical mass of highly enriched uranium. On the other end of the cylinder was another sub-critical mass of uranium. The distance separating the two sub-critical masses prevented an explosion. Attached to one end of the cylinder was a propellant to which, was fashioned a detonator that once detonated would force one of the sub-critical masses of uranium into the other forming a super-critical mass that in a millionth of a second would result in a nuclear explosion.

The device was ready except for the detonator. It was the Imam's responsibility to deliver the device to Miami. The timing was perfect. There was disagreement as regards port security in the United States. It had made all the headlines. The instruction for assembling the detonator was in Steve's hands. He merely had to pick up the device from Miami, travel with it to Chicago and keep it in a 120 dollar per month storage bin waiting for the proper timing to put it to use.

CHAPTER 27

FLORIDA

Bart:

Steve made about 200 miles on his first evening's trip to Florida. He stopped at a motel and left the next morning to arrive at his destination. He had very important business to implement in Miami. When he arrived he met Bart of Hollywood, Florida.

Bart was a little man, short and stocky with a dark complexion, dark brown eyes, thick bushy eyebrows and an L-shaped scar on his chin all of which gave him the appearance of a Mafia hit man. He was born in the United States of Muslim parents. He resided with his wife and two children in Hollywood, just north of Miami. He worked for a British company who ran the port in Miami, and had a working knowledge of the arrival of containers shipped in from all over the world.

Miami is one of the busiest ports in the United States. Each year there are approximately thirteen million shipping containers coming into U.S. ports with about one-half arriving from overseas. Only five percent of containers that arrive are inspected. The rest undergo absolutely no scrutiny. Needless to say an attack through a port could cost horrendous loss of life. The terrorists know this. Once a container arrives it is taken by truck to any destination in America further compounding the threat. Steve was well aware of this soft underbelly of American inattentiveness and he and his well coordinated group, organized at the top under the direction of the Imam, were ready to take advantage of this security lapse.

"So Bart, bring me up to date," said Steve.

"The container is in. It'll be loaded on an eighteen wheeler tomorrow morning and head north. The same driver will deliver it to the same location he always does. He's made that run many times. After four hours on the road he'll stop at a truck stop and have lunch."

"How do you know he'll stop there?" asked Steve.

"He always does."

"What if he doesn't."

"Then plan B goes into effect."

"There's not enough of us to carry out plan B," noted Steve, shaking his head.

"Not to worry. I have two more of us at the truck stop. They'll be there to help in case he stops there, but if he doesn't we'll call them on the cell in code and they'll leave the stop and follow us. There will be four of us in three cars to hijack his truck if that's what we have to do. But I tell you, the chance of his not stopping is zero. We've been watching this guy for over six months, and he always stops."

"Okay, refresh my memory about what we do at the truck stop," said Steve.

"The driver will go in and have lunch. One reason I'm sure he will stop is because he's very friendly with a waitress there. He spends at least an hour eating and talking and reading the paper. We'll park our cars as close as we can to his truck. Then we'll open the container locks, get inside and pull the gift for the infidels out. It'll be right at the truck back door entrance which will face the woods, so there should be no one there to see what we do. One strong guy could handle it, but with all of us there it'll be no problem. We'll bring it to your car. We act like we belong there. Then you're off to the party."

"How do you know what to pull out of the truck," asked Steve.

My contact told me exactly what the box will look like. It has special marks. Only me and one other guy know which box it is."

Steve wondered at the complexity and brilliance of an organization that has so compartmentalized its work. The pieces fit together like a puzzle and each puzzle piece only knows about itself and its part in the overall plan. "Okay, Bart where do I meet you tomorrow?"

"Right here. Same time. You'll follow me to where the trucks leave the port. You can't go inside, so we'll park near the exit from the port. I know just about when he'll leave the port. Then we'll pull in behind his truck and follow him. I've been through this one hundred times in my mind. We can't miss."

"You're sure? This whole thing depends on getting that box out of the truck and delivering it to Chicago in the next few days."

"A piece of cake, as the infidels say, Steve."

"Okay, Bart. I'll see you in the morning."

The next morning he met Bart. Everything went just as Bart had said it would.

"Are you going to tell me what the gift for the infidels is, where it came from and where it's going, Steve?"

"Bart, you know better than that. I'm in charge of this operation, but even I'm not told some of the planning details." I'm in charge of the operation in this country. That I know about. If you want to know more just read the papers, my good man, or keep your eye on the boob tube."

Steve left for Chicago with his cargo on board. It would be placed in a storage bin. The bin was empty, having been rented by Steve six months ago. When he rented it, he paid for twelve months in advance. He was careful to disguise his appearance and used a false name and address. With the advance payment it was not likely anyone would bother him for a year.

The unsuspecting truck driver took off for his destination unaware that he was playing a part in what Steve hoped would soon be the worst days in the history of the United States of America.

CHAPTER 28

The Trojan Horses:

Ben left Steve's apartment and went back to his dormitory. He focused his mind on the math problem and would give it one more try before he sought help from professor Jamison. He put the boxes he received from Steve in his suitcases and hid them in the closet. Then he sat down at his desk and opened his math book. The cloud was still there. Ben realized that his failure to solve the problem was a factor in not being able to dissipate the cloud and interfere with his mind. He had to solve it. He worked a full hour, but he remained unsuccessful. He had no choice. He would speak to his professor tomorrow morning. That evening he had difficulty sleeping, waking up often because of horrible dreams.

The next morning he went to his professor's office. His door was open. He was sitting at his desk, cluttered with papers. Behind him was a large portable blackboard filled with complicated mathematical symbols known only to a few.

"Excuse me, professor. I need help on a problem and wondered if you have a few minutes to work with me?"

Jamison looked up at Ben over his reading glasses perched on the end of his large nose. With his baldhead, he had the appearance of an aging nerd. "Oh, Ben, it's you. Sure, what can I do for you?" Jamison considered Ben the most brilliant student he had instructed in thirty years of teaching, so he was curious at Ben's call for help.

"It's the extra credit problem, professor."

"Which one?" asked Jamison.

"The last one of the two," answered Ben in a whisper.

"The professor smiled and nodded his head. "Let me tell you something, Ben. In the thirty years I've been teaching, I could count on one hand the number of times a student has even attempted that problem. I keep using it because it has a trap, and everyone that tries to work it falls into it."

"I was thinking that the answer in the book is wrong," said Ben, his leg shaking in the usual rhythmic manner.

Jamison laughed. "If anyone could find a wrong answer in the book, it would be you, Ben. Here, let me see your work."

Jamison turned to the third page of Ben's four pages of work. Ben could see a smile forming on the professor's face. "Just as I thought, Ben. Would you like me to give you a clue?"

"I'd appreciate that, professor. It bothers me when I can't solve a problem. I get confused and I lose concentration."

"Okay look at this operation. You have derived a very complex division. The numerator is fine. Check the denominator."

"I've done that many times, and I can't find anything wrong."

"Okay, do you want me to tell you, Ben?"

Ben felt himself becoming upset. The cloud was still there, but at the same time, he could feel the fire rising in his belly. His mind was becoming confused. He had much to do this evening and had to get hold of himself. Jamison could see the changing expression on Ben's face, and he noted Ben's shaking leg. I have to get over this, said Ben to himself. I can't let math do this to me if I want to be a mathematician.

"Ben, get hold of yourself. Let me tell you now that this problem has no solution. It is a trick problem. The denominator here on page three is very complex, and has been derived by a complicated series of steps. That's the problem, Ben. If you carefully dissect the derivation of the denominator, you would find that your derivation reveals a term that equals zero. When I first tried to work this problem many years ago, I failed also. So you are dividing by zero, Ben. What happens when you divide by zero?"

"Of course, of course. What have I done? Division by zero is undefined. No wonder! My answer is finite. Divide any number by decreasing numbers, and as the divisor approaches zero as a limit the answer approaches infinity. Clever; I was fooled. But where is my mistake? Where did I screw up?" Ben stared at the professor with wide eyes. He looked down at the problem and turned to the preceding pages. Then he looked at Jamison again, and Jamison could not help but notice a look of dismay in Ben's face.

"Ben, get hold of yourself. It's okay. The mistake is right here," said Jamison pointing with his pencil.

Ben stared silently where Jamison had pointed. After a few moments, Ben said calmly, "Yes professor, I see…I see…stupid of me."

"Ben, the greatest mathematicians of the world have made similar mistakes. You are the most brilliant student I have ever worked with, and I speak from all those years of dealing with students."

"You are a great mathematician, professor," said Ben in a monotone.

"You're wrong, Ben. I am an average mathematician. I am a good learner. I can learn what the great mathematicians have taught us. However, I have never come up with an original mathematical thought. I could not be a Laplace. I could never be a Newton or Leibniz. I could never be a Fourier or Gauss, Galois, Euler. These are true mathematicians. They reveal God's secrets."

God, thought Ben. Ah, yes. That's what Steve said. Allah! There's where I will understand all mathematics. He smiled—a far-away look on his face.

"Ben, what are you thinking? Snap out of it. You are not the average mathematician. You could do great things. You could be like the great mathematical pioneers I mentioned, and I've never said that about any other student I ever taught."

Ben shook his head. "Thank you for the kind words, professor. Thank you for the help."

"I'll see you in class, Ben."

"Goodbye, professor."

Ben went through the rest of his classes in almost a hypnotic trance. His mind was blank. He finished at 4:00, went back to his room. The others would be starting their work today, he thought.

In the meantime, Jenny started her tasks earlier. She decided to go to the loop at 4:00 when it would be crowded with people leaving offices and heading home. She parked her car in the underground Grant Park parking garage. She decided that a good place to go would be the Union Station where thousands of people would be catching trains. She was dressed in slacks and a plain blouse with a thin windbreaker jacket. She did not wear any make up. She carried a small purse with a shoulder strap and her weapons inside.

Joe started his activities in a large shopping center on sixty-first street. He disseminated his ingredients in at least twenty stores. Then he went home to plan the next six days activities.

The residents of a bustling city continued on, little dreaming what awaited them.

CHAPTER 29

Victim number one:

Steve returned from Florida after an all night trip. He drove to his rented storage facility and left his cargo inside. One wire protruding through the box needed to be connected to the detonator start mechanism. Then the mere pressing of a trigger would propel one U-235 into the other resulting in a nuclear explosion.

He drove back home and decided to relax the rest of the day.

The next morning Steve woke up, left his apartment about nine o'clock and drove to Michigan Avenue. He carried the daily ration of three aerosols and three envelopes and a small scissors in his pocket. He started at Chicago Avenue and worked his way south down Michigan Avenue toward the Loop. As he disseminated the weapons he also shopped. It took him four hours to complete his work, so he had a liesure lunch and walked back to the parking lot, retrieved his car and drove home where he would plan the next six days activities.

Joe faithfully and eagerly completed his task in the allotted time. He spent two full days at the Museum of Science and Industry. The facility was crowded with people visiting a major exhibit.

Jenny, assigned to the Loop, concentrated much of her activity at Macys formerly known as Marshall Fields, a century old, premier department store. She also spent time at the downtown Hilton, filled with business travelers and conventioneers. She made a second trip to Union Station.

The work of the Holy Warriors had not yet been completed when their handiwork was making itself felt within the Chicago metropolitan area. Carrie Harper, a forty-one year old housewife and mother of two, resided in Arlington Heights, Illinois, a northwest suburb of Chicago.

She did all of her shopping at Old Orchard shopping center and was rummaging through some chidren's clothes when invisible anthrax spores fell on the back of her hand. She never knew it, but these spores landed on an unnoticed insect bite that she had received a few days before. Within two days she began scratching, and when she looked down at her hand all she noted was a small red spot. Thinking nothing of it, she went about her usual activities and scratched on an intermittent basis. A few days later the small spot had become a larger bump, and then filled with clear fluid. She covered it with a band aid. When her husband returned from work that evening, she took off the band aid, showed him her hand and said, "What do you think this is?"

He studied the lesion and said, "I bet you got a spider bite."

"Oh, gross," she exclaimed. "I told you we should get an exterminator in this house. Better me then one of the kids, I guess."

"Sure, go ahead and call them, I don't care. That'll heal up okay. They all do. Maybe you're a little allergic to spider bites."

But soon the fluid filled bump broke open, and the center began to turn black. At the same time the skin around the black area began to swell. There was no pain. The lesion now was much greater in size. The appearance frightened Ms. Harper and she called her doctor and insisted on a same day appointment as the sore was getting larger and blacker and more swollen.

The doctor studied the lesion. "That's a nasty bite, Ms. Harper. I'm sure your husband is right, some spider got to you probably in your sleep. But you're getting a lot of swelling and infection; the black skin is dead skin. You see, when the spider bites, it leaves a toxin, which in your case has killed quite a bit of the skin and caused infection, so I better put you on antibiotics. He wrote a prescription for 500 milligram Ampicillin tablets. "Swollow one of these with water three times per day." He gave her a ten day supply. "Rest your hand and arm. Keep it in this sling during the day. When you sleep, keep it elevated on a pillow. In a week or two it should be fine."

Ms. Harper was lucky. In cutaneous anthrax, a disease that has a twenty percent mortality rate, she would survive, even though the diagnosis was incorrect as was the treatment. The lesion would heal. She was the first. How many more would there be? When would someone establish a diagnosis?

CHAPTER 30

Victim number two:

Jessie Warren wouldn't miss the game for anything. His kid brother, Mason, had been All-State in high school, and he was now a starting freshman on the Northwestern University basketball team. Jessie had an excellent seat twenty rows up from the court. He was on line with the center jump-all circle. His girl friend and some of his former schoolmates, who watched Mason grow up in the same Chicago neighborhood, accompanied him to the game. Northwestern University was turning out good basketball teams, as they were the recipient of some of Chicago's premier High School basketball players who perfected their craft on the playgrounds of Chicago.

Jessie was a security guard at Covenant Hospital. He was tall and lean with short, curly black hair, an upright straight-backed walk, and large pearly-white teeth that lit up his smiling face. He liked his job dealing with hospital security, but was considering a try for the Chicago Police Department. He needed one more year of school and was attending evening classes at Oakton Junior College in the northwest suburbs.

Things were going well, but Jessie's good fortune would soon change. He would learn that there were all kinds of variables that could disrupt one's plans. In Jessie's case, the variable was the misfortune to have his great seat lie under a man man who was sitting in the second level of the basketball stadium armed with biological terror weapons and spraying them over the balcony railing.

Smallpox spores descended downward, jostling nitrogen and oxygen molecules and finally occupying the atmosphere adjacent to Jessie's nostrils. They would start on their path to destruction when Jessie inhaled them and they landed in his respiratory tract; some landed in his mouth as he ate his hotdog and others fell on his clothing. These latter would arrive at his home later.

The smallpox spores that landed on Jessie's lung cells would quickly be activated. They would then replicate (divide and form more virus). Then they would leave the lung cells and circulate in Jessie's blood stream. When they found scavenger cells of the body, circulating in the blood stream and also fixed in different tissues, they would park there and set up shop. And when they were ready, they would leave these cells, circulate in the blood stream again, and finally cause disease.

This stimulation of Jessie's immune system caused a fever, which came to his aid in an attempt to gain advantage over the invading virus. An elevated temperature suppresses the virus's ability to reproduce itself. Jessie's hypothalamus, sitting at the base of the brain, is the body's thermostat. The invading virus and the body tissues liberate biochemical sustances, which circulate in Jessie's blood stream. When the hypothalamus detected these substances, it told Jessie's body to make more heat. Heat, you see, supresses viruses.

Jessie felt this effect while at work one day. He developed an elevated temperature accompanied by muscle aches and weakness. He felt light headed and dizzy. The symptoms seemed to be increasing in intensity. He had to leave his post and told his supervisor that something was wrong; he didn't feel right and was too weak to stand. His supervisor accompanied him to the Emergency Department and registered him at the front desk. Then Jessie was interviewed by the triage nurse. She took his temperature (102.3), and she gave him a cursory examination. She had him wait in the waiting room for a short while. Soon Jessie was called into an examining room where he was seen by Dr. Pollard.

Pollard recognized his patient attired in his security uniform. He picked up his chart. "Hello, Mr. Warren. What brings you to the Emergency Department?"

"I got a fever and I feel weak and achy."

"How long have you had these symptoms?" Pollard inquired.

"I started feeling weak and achy yesterday. Today it got worse."

"Any cough or sore throat?"

"No."

"Any pain or burning when you urinate?"

"No."

"Have you been around anyone sick?"

"Not that I know of."

"Have you been in good health, Mr. Warren?"

"Oh yeah. Never had no big problem."

"Any allergies to any medicines?"

"No."

Pollard, noting that his patient's voice was weak reflecting a true illness, continued with a full medical history and a thorough physical examination. It was essentially negative except for his elevated temperature and a diffuse faint rash over his trunk that had the appearance of measles. He also noted a few punctate red spots that he thought were petechia (small red skin spots caused by minute hemorrhages and seen with infectious diseases as well as other medical problems). "How long have you had this rash?" asked Pollard.

"What rash, doctor?"

"Here on your body."

Jessie looked down. "I don't know. I don't see much."

"Have you ever had measles?"

"No. My mother said I got all my shots when I was a kid. That's measles too, ain't it?"

"That's right. If you got all your shots you should have gotten the measles shot too. I want to get a blood count on you. I'll do it right away."

"Sure, doc."

The complete blood count was unremarkable except for a reduced total white blood cell count with increased lymphocytes. This ruled out many potential problems, and zeroed in to the diagnosis of a systemic, or generalized viral infection.

Pollard approached the patient with the blood count report. "It looks like you've got a virus, Mr. Warren."

"So what do I do, doc?"

"I think it would be okay to go home, get to bed, drink plenty of fluids and take two tylenols three times a day if your temperature stays more than 102. Everything points to a virus. You should be better in a few days. Don't come back to work until your fever's been normal for at least twenty-four hours."

"Thanks, doc, I'll do that."

Jessie drove home and went to bed. He did not return to work the next day. His parents called his apartment and there was no answer. His girl friend did the same. They called work and were told that Jessie was sent home with a virus and had not yet returned to work. When they called again and still received no answer, his father went to his apartment, let himself in and found Jessie cold, unresponsive and lifeless lying in his bed. He was rushed via ambulance to Covenant. Amanda Galinski saw him this time. She listened to his heart in a vain attempt to hear heart sounds, checked his pupils and found them fixed and dilated. She declared him dead.

She spoke with the family and stressed that this was a very unusual death in a healthy young man. Her best guess was that he most likey died of a viral infection that involved the brain causing a fulminating encephalitis or brain infection. Nothing could have been done. It would take an autopsy to find out exactly what happened. The distraught parents consented.

Pollard was not working that day, but Amanda told him about his patient when he arrived at work the next day. He was distraught. What did I miss, he thought. He went to his office and sat at his desk, staring at the textbooks on the wall. It must have been an encephalitis, he thought. God, how could that have been predicted? Another possibility was that the infection resulted in an unusual complication which caused the patient to bleed to death internally. However, his platellet count was normal on the blood count. So that probably rules it out. Unless, of course, it developed precipitously. And so it went, over and over in Pollard's mind; the same kind of thinking that goes on in every doctor's mind when there is an unexpected, and untoward outcome; running down a list of possibilities. This was not the first time this had happened, and it wouldn't be the last, but he would never be able to not let it affect him. The pursuit of perfection in medicine was as elusive as it was in any profession or any other field of endeavor.

CHAPTER 31

Victim number three:

Wilson, Harmon, Alban, and Davis, one of the premier law firms in the city of Chicago, occupy the top four floors of the 810 Wacker Drive building. James Harmon, born and reared in Chicago, attended Northwestern University Law School. He graduated in 1993, and together with his classmate, Al Wilson, started a law firm concentrating on corporate law. Years later, after some brilliant mergers, they were a 220 person practice.

Harmon was one of the quintessential baby boomer success stories. He had a mansion in River Forest, a western suburb of Chicago, a family with four grown children, lots of money in the bank, plenty of political influence in the city and an appearance to match the success he had achieved: tall, athletic, good looking, a full head of graying, wavy hair and an air of supreme confidence. He was "the man with the golden touch." But none of this would help him today.

He left work at five o'clock. The good news was that he would not be bringing home his briefcase. He contemplated relaxation in an empty house alone with his wife. But he had the misfortune to stop at the newspaper kiosk in the Union Station, and purchased one-half dozen of his favorite candy bars, and the latest Sports Illustrated magazine.

What Harmon had no way of knowing was that Jenny had just passed this way, and in her hand she had a small envelope whose edge had been cut. As she reached over with her left hand to hold up a paper and read the headline, with her other hand she sprinkled some of the weaponized anthrax on the candy bars and the magazine display. Then she walked on to look for another good target.

Harmon never even saw the fine powder waft upward, and when he picked up the magazine it disrupted the particles and sent them in a trajectory toward his face, which at that time was intent on reading the front cover. He paid for his purchase and caught the train heading west to River Forest.

Even before he boarded the train, the anthrax spores were enveloped by alveolar macrophages (scavenger immune cells in the lung air sacs) and transported to mediastinal (cardiac area) and pleural (lung covering area) lymph nodes. Now the spores had the perfect envronment to germinate, and they sprung to life. In Harmon's case this took only a matter of five days. The two protien toxins lead to the characteristic features of the deadly disease: hemorrhage in the infected lymph nodes; infection around the heart and hemorrhagic pleural effusions (bloody fluid around the lungs). From this, there resulted a showering of bacteria into the blood stream causing infectious spread, sepsis and diffuse organ failure.

The initial clinical manifestations of Harmon's inhalation anthrax was fever, chills and a nonproductive cough. This was followed by some chest pain. He was in his office when his symptoms became worrisome, and he went to the closest hospital emergency room. He was examined and found to have a temperature of 100.6. The examining physician heard some rales (crackles) in his right lung suggesting fluid congestion and told the patient that he was possibly coming down with a pneumonia.

"Can I get some antibiotics and take care of this thing?" said Harmon.

"You could, but I'd be reluctant to do that without some tests."

"What kind of tests are you talking about" asked Harmon.

"Well, I'd like to get a chest x-ray and see what it shows. Also a blood count would be a good idea."

"How long would that take, doctor?"

"Are you in a hurry?"

"Well, yeah. My law firm is in the middle of a very important deal and we're due at a meeting soon."

"I probably could get it all in one-half hour."

"And you'll let me know right away?"

"Yes sir."

"Okay do it then."

When the results were in, the doctor reported to Harmon that his complete blood count showed an elevated white blood count with a preponderance of neutrophils (blood scavenger cells that fight bacterial infection). This meant that there was definitely a bacterial infection in play. His chest x-ray did indeed show what appeared to be a patch of pneumonia in the right lung base.

"You do have an early pneumonia, Mr. Harmon."

"Damn! How the hell did I get that? Okay, I'll take the antibiotics and go home and rest until I'm better."

"That could be done, but it's not the best idea," said the doctor. "I would want to start you on intravenous antibiotics in the hospital after taking some blood cultures."

"You're talking inpatient?"

"Yes."

"Look, doctor. I know you're just doing your job, and I appreciate it, but here's what I have to do. I have to be at this meeting. I'll take the antibiotics, I'll go home after the meeting, and if I'm not feeling better in forty-eight hours, or if I get worse, I'll come right back."

"Okay, Mr. Harmon. I don't recommend this approach, but I can't tie you to the bed. You'd be better off in the hospital where you can be closely monitored."

"I appreciate that. Doctor, but I'll take the risk and watch myself like a hawk."

"Okay, the patient is always the boss. Take these three times a day. Start now. Here's some samples and a prescription, but the deal is, before you take the medicine and go, I'll take a quick blood culture. That's so we will be able to identify the bacteria that is causing the pneumonia in case you don't respond to the antibiotic."

"Sure, thanks, doctor, that makes sense. I appreciate you working with me on this."

Harmon struggled through the meeting and the trip back home. He went to bed, and by the next morning he was weaker, his breathing was faster, his temperature was higher, and his wife became frightened over his confusion and blue lips. She called 911 and the paramedic ambulance rushed him to West Suburban Hospital where he was admitted to Intensive Care. An endotracheal tube was inserted. A respirator was attached to the tube to assist the patient's breathing. Intravenous antibiotics and oxygen were administered and a priest was called to deliver the last rites. Harmon expired twelve hours after he was placed in Intensive care. Why, wondered his wife? Why did a healthy man die?

The doctors approached the grieving wife. "Would you consent to an autopsy, Ms. Harmon?"

"Yes, yes," she said. Then after controlling her sobs, she added, "We've got to know what happened."

CHAPTER 32

All hell breaks loose:

A week had passed, and the Holy Warrior Tojan Horses had completed their work. Unusual cases began to show up in Chicago and suburbs. Physicians were misdiagnosing in emergency rooms and offices all over the Chicago metropolitan area, but two clever physicians in a northwest suburban medical center, Dr. Goodman and Dr. Weiss, saw the lesion the likes of which they had never seen before, suspected the worst including cutaneous anthrax in one of their patients, consulted with google, saw pictures identical to the lesion and took the patient to a dermatologist's office and asked for an immediate punch biopsy at the edge of the lesion. The dermatologist agreed, and they brought the specimen to the pathology department and requested a stat analysis. Their worst fears were realized; cutaneous anthrax was proven. A complete history was taken from the patient. She had not been out of the country, she never worked with animal skin or furs and she had not deviated from her usual routine for many months. The Chicago Public health department was alerted, and so was the Centers for Disease Control (CDC) in Atlanta.

That same day the news about the cutaneous anthrax found in the northwest suburbs of Chicago was broadcast all over the country featuring interviews with Drs. Goodman and Weiss.

Jason Pollard was watching the evening news, and he leaped out of his chair.

"What happened?" asked his alarmed wife, Sarah.

"They diagnosed a case of cutaneous anthrax in a northwest suburb. The patient had not been out of the country, and had no risk factors. They suspect bio-terrorism."

"Oh my God," said Sarah as she cradled one of her children in her arms. "That patient who died on me! Remember I told you about him. I saw him just a week or so ago. He was toxic and had a rash with petechiae. I diagnosed him as a viral infection. But—.Jesus, maybe it was smallpox! It could be a virulent form. Oh my God, I've been exposed. The kids, you, the whole Emergency Department has been exposed!"

Sarah saw a fear erupt on her husband's face the likes of which she had never seen. He reached into a desk drawer and took out a medical staff phone book with doctors' home phone listings. He looked up the phone number of Dr. Schwartz, the chief of pathology and rushed to the phone.

"Karl, this is Jason. We have an emergency."

"What is it, Jason?"

"Have you done the autopsy on patient Jessie Warren?"

"No. It's on the schedule for tomorrow. Bill's doing it."

"It can't wait, Karl. Did you hear the news tonight?"

"No. What's up?"

"They diagnosed a case of cutaneous anthrax in the suburbs. They're pretty sure it's bio-terrorism. I think Warren may have died of smallpox. We can't wait. Let's autopsy him tonight. I'll meet you there. Many of us have been exposed. The country has got to know."

Schwartz could easily hear the fear in Pollard's tremulous voice. There was silence for a brief period. Then Schwartz said, "Okay, I'm going, but Jason, you've got a problem unless you received a vaccination…"

Jason interrupted, "Only as a kid."

"Okay good. We'll still need another vaccination if this is smallpox. Get moving. I have to call the health department and tell them we'll be coming with a possible pox fluid specimen…"

"Hold it, Karl. When I saw him he didn't have any pox."

"We'll see if he's developed any since. Let's go."

Schwartz called the health department. The lines were busy. Now that the word about bio-terrorissm was out, people all over the country were trying to call Chicago. Chicagoans were trying to call relatives and friends. Very few could get through.

They arrived at the hospital morgue and suited up with mask, gown and gloves. A careful external body review by Schwartz demonstrated the rash and petechiae that Pollard had seen before. When he and Pollard turned over the body, they found early pox formation in a few areas.

"Look, Jason. You could be right," exclaimed Schwartz loudly.

Whatever fluid was able to be expressed was put in a small test tube, and several of the lesions were also taken. Then a complete autopsy was performed and cytology specimens were taken of all internal organs.

Schwartz tried to call the health department again. He still couldn't get through. "Go home, Jason, I'll have to drive there and take the samples myself. There's someone there twenty-four hours a day."

"Thanks Karl. I really appreciate everything you've done."

"This will be a rush job. We should have the answer tomorrow."

Pollard tried to call his wife. He couldn't get through. He drove home. The best he could get was a few hours of restless sleep.

By the next morning, after Jessie Warren's case was confirmed as smallpox, and the news was out, cases of smallpox and anthrax, both cutaneous and inhalational, were being reported all over the country. It became apparent that the epicenter was Chicago. All other news was relegated to the back pages of the newspapers. TV commentators spoke only of the sudden threat to the United States and the world. People were advised to report any suspicious symptoms. Information about the diseases was being broadcast day and night. Everyday more and more cases were diagnosed now that physicians were alerted to the possibility. The CDC was working in conjunction with the Chicago Health Department and were doing patient contact tracing. Centers for smallpox and anthrax immunization were set up in all hospitals. All contacts with proven patients were to be immunized first. Jason and his family received smallpox and anthrax immunization. As a member of the Covenant Emergency Department, Amanda Galinski was also immunized. All police and health care workers were to be immunized, but this task was difficult in that delivery was often delayed. Chicago streets and avenues were becoming deserted. The Chicago economy was grinding to a halt. People who were not infected were instructed to stay home until further notice as it became clear that a double bio-terrorist attack was in progress. The CDC kept records of all reported cases so as to determine if there was any evidence of a rising or falling rate. No one could know when it would end.

The autopsy of attorney Harmon confirmed a diagnosis of inhalation anthrax.

It would not be long before there were reports of deleterious effects of the multiple immunizations including some deaths. But there was no choice. They had to be continued.

All traffic into and out of O'Hare field ground to a halt except for approved emergency trips taken by the Federal Government, and private planes with an important reason to make the trip. Train traffic stopped.

Hospitals were filling fast with urgent cases. All Intensive Care units were filled to capacity. Other sections of hospitals were converted as best as possible to mimic Intensive Care units. Special isolation wards were set up. Emergency medical personnel and the entire medical community were beginning to run on empty.

National Guard was activated and were immunized and assisted police in patrolling the streets where some looting was taking place.

CHAPTER 33

Amanda falls victim:

Amanda woke up every morning at 6:00. She was always able to depend on her internal clock. When she awakened she would have a small breakfast consisting of cereal and milk. She never drank coffee, as it made her nauseaous, and this caused her to often wonder as to coffee's popularity in the world.

This morning, however, she awakened at 5:00. She did not feel well, so she remained awake. She also realized that she had no appetite. She was dizzy when she sat up, her head was throbbing with pain and her body ached all over. God, she thought, what am I coming down with? Her temperature was 100.6, which was elevated for this time of the morning. She checked her body and her face in the mirror, and did not find any pox or rash. With what was happening in Chicago, she knew she should not go to work. At ten minutes to 7:00 she called Dr. Pollard and told him of her dilemma.

"Stay home, Amanda. You're doing the right thing. There's enough risk around here already, not to mention how vulnerable you might be with all that's going on. Let's pray you're not coming down with one of the twin curses. Even if you do, I'm pretty sure the immunizations we've all had will keep it mild. Are you taking the Cipro?"

"Yes."

"Good. Do you have any cough?"

"No."

"That's great. It's probably not inhalation anthrax. Any signs of pox?"

"No, I don't see any."

"Any rash at all?"

"None."

"Okay just stay home, keep well hydrated, get plenty of bed rest and keep me posted. Please call me morning, afternoon and night with a report. The phones are loosening up now, so you should be able to get through, or call my cell."

"I will, Jason."

Amanda's symptoms progressed that day and the next. By early the next evening her temperature peaked at 102.8. She took a few tylenol for the discomfort and elevated temperature. The third day she did notice three pox on her abdomen, and reported to Pollard.

"That's all, just three. Are you sure?"

"I even checked my backside in the mirror. There's none there. The three are all I can find."

"Okay, that's a good sign. I'm confident that you were already beginning to incubate the virus when you got the vaccination, and that's what's minimizing the damn thing. Keep calling. We need you, Amanda. Have you got enough food there?"

"I'm fine, Jason.

"Is there anything else you need?"

"Nope, I'm all set. I've read the Emergency Department manual two times."

"That's a good use of your time, Amanda. Keep up the fine work."

The next two days, Amanda remained unchanged in terms of the number of Pox. She was also feeling better as far as her clinical symptoms were concerned. She reported to Pollard.

"You'll be fine in a few days, Amanda. We've all been praying for you. As soon as the pox have crusted over you can come back to work. Hallelujah!"

That evening her mother called. Amanda's answer to her mother's how are you was, "I'm fine I feel great, but I just got over something."

"What?" asked her alarmed mother.

"A mild case of Smallpox."

"Oh my God! Richard," she screamed.

"Calm down, mother. I'm cured. I'm fine. I'm going back to work soon."

CHAPTER 34

Ultimatum:

It was now two and a half weeks since the Holy Warrior Trojan Horses had completed their task. Twelve hundred people had died and twenty-six hundred survived their illnesses. The great majority were from Chicago and the surrounding area. The number of cases had not yet leveled off. Extensive interviewing of surviving patients did not come up with a single location where the terrorists had operated. It was clear that there was a widespread dissemination beyond the capability of one person to accomplish. There had to be multiple terrorists in action. There were a few areas of the city where there seemed to be a number of cases more than would be expected by a random accounting.

Suddenly, a masked and unknown Islamist spokesperson appeared on TV. He stood in front of a black background. Bedecked in spotless white apparel, and a facial covering, he rambled on about the success of the world struggle against the apostates, promising more to come and assuring his followers of a glorious and total victory. Then he took credit for the "attack on the sin-city of Chicago in the land of the Great Satan." He praised the Holy Warriors who carried out the brilliant attack. Then a further warning: "All apostates should know that the big attack in Chicago will soon be coming, and it will make what has already happened pale in comparison." Then he paused for a few seconds and said, "There is only one thing that could stop the coming attack. What there are left of American troops, down to the last man, will evacuate all Holy Muslim lands. You have one month from the date of this broadcast to develop evacuation plans."

CHAPTER 35

Epiphany:

Amanda Galinski had been working almost to the point of exhaustion. Her father, Richard was likewise doing the same on the streets of Chicago. One day he drove his patrol car to Covenant and found his daughter at work.

"How are you, Amanda? We've been worried about you."

"I'm safe, dad. I can't get over how naive I've been. We are at war, and I never realized it."

"That's okay, Amanda. You are not alone."

"What are you doing, dad?"

"We're working with the FBI."

"Any clues?"

"Not really, but there are two areas of the city where there are more cases than the statisticians figure there should be. One is on the south side, and the other is the area around Evanston."

"Evanston?" said Amanda.

"Yes."

Then she pulled a memory out of her brain that had long been buried. Maloney's! Alan Kanter, Northwestern, Gauss, Gauss and the Cipros. He lied about what they were. Why? "Dad, I have a crazy thought," said Amanda, a look off fear and horror on her face that her father instantly recognized.

Richard had learned from past experience that Amanda's hunches had an amazing way of bearing fruit. "What is it?" he exclaimed nervously

Amanda told her father about the evening she took the three nurses to dinner at Maloney's. "There were four young men students from Northwestern, dad. They were sitting at a table next to ours. One of them, the youngest who they called Gauss, had some pills in his wallet that fell out on the table. When one of the other students asked him what they were, he said cold pills. But they weren't. I'm certain! I was able to see exactly what they were. They were Cipros; I'm sure. And don't forget this was before the attacks. This guy with the Cipro's was a strange one."

"Couldn't he be taking them for a legitimate reason?"

"Sure. It's used for urinary tract infections, but that's pretty rare in a young man."

"What you're saying is, he could he have been using it, or keeping it available because he knew what was about to happen."

"I know it sounds far fetched, dad, but it just came to my mind. It's just one of those coincidences that I'm sure has no value."

"I pay attention to your hunches, Amanda. Anyhow we have absolutely no leads at all. We're groping in the dark and have to follow any lead no matter how crazy it sounds. We're working on a deadline imposed by a madman. By the way, did you say his name is Gauss?"

"That's what his friends call him, but I doubt if it really is. I would bet his classmates named him that because he's probably a math wiz. Do you know who Gauss was, dad?"

"Let me fool you, Amanda. Gauss was the mathematician who when he was six years old was sitting in class when his teacher told all the students to add up all the numbers from one to one hundred. The teacher did it because he had a lot of work to do and he figured that would keep the students busy the entire hour. Gauss did it in a few seconds because he reasoned that one and 100 equals 101. Two and ninety-nine equals 101. Three and ninety-eight equals 101, etcetera. Since there were fifty pairs the answer was fifty times 101, or 5,050."

"Dad, you never cease to amaze me."

"And you never stop amazing me, Amanda. I'm going to follow up this lead of yours. Do you know the guy's real name?" He began rolling his antique marbles in his pocket. "No, but I remember his friend's name, Alan Kanter."

"Is that a C or a K?"

"I don't know, I just remember him saying it."

"Okay. I'll alert the FBI. We'll track down this lead. I love you, Amanda. Please take care of yourself."

"You too, dad, you're the one who's entering the hornet's nest. Please don't do anything foolish. I love you."

"I love you too, Amanda."

CHAPTER 36

William Vladic, FBI:

Galinski reported Amanda's conversation about Gauss to the FBI man working with him. William Vladic was a senior agent for the bureau who had been assigned to the Chicago office for the last ten years. Galinski enjoyed working with him as he was all business, and had no problem putting in sixteen hour days. Vladic was an attorney, a graduate of the Chicago Kent College of Law located in downtown Chicago. He was fifty years of age, five feet ten inches tall with a salt and pepper gray beard and a black mustache. Vladic was always well-dressed in a suit and white shirt, but often without a tie. He had just completed a twenty year stint as an army reserve JAG officer with a rank of Lieutenant Colonel. He had been called up to serve during Desert Storm, and had strong opinions about what to do with terrorists. As soon as Galinski finished the story about Gauss, Vladic got up from the lunch table and said, "Let's move our ass."

"Where are we going?" asked Galinski.

"Northwestern."

"The school is closed."

"I know. I'm sure the students are all home, but we need information about this Gauss character. We need his real name, so let's see if we can find out where this Alan Kanter lives. We'll go see him and get what we need."

"Man, you don't let any grass grow under your feet, do you?" asked Galinski.

"Never did, never will."

The Northwestern campus, just as most of the Chicago area, was like a ghost town. Commerce in the town of Evanston had shut down. People were doing everything they could to not congregate in crowds, fearing that the person who would bump into them in the streets was the one who would pass on smallpox or anthrax. Families stayed together within their own homes, only venturing out to get food in large supermarkets. National Guard soldiers were on the streets, and controlled the crowds coming for food. People whose last names started with certain letters of the alphabet were told what day they could shop for food. Looting stopped after a few were shot with the intention of wounding. There was a siege atmosphere, but there was no choice.

Galinski and Vladic went to the administration building only to find it locked. Vladic looked around and saw a Northwestern security guard walking toward them. The guard said, "Can I help you gentlemen?"

"We need to get in that building," said Vladic even before the guard finished the sentence.

The hesitation of the guard caused Vladic to put his FBI badge in the guard's face. "This is government business. Open the door now."

"The scowl on Vladic's face and the intensity of his words were enough for the guard. He did as he was told.

"Is there anybody here?" asked Vladic.

"Not that I know of, sir."

"Where would I find the list of students and their home addresses."

"I would imagine it's on the computer," said the guard.

"We'd probably need a code to get in," said Galinski.

"Shit, you're right, I'm sure," said Vladic. Then he turned to the guard. Do you know where the boss of this school lives?"

"Yeah, the dean lives in the house right off of the north end of the campus."

"Show us where," said Vladic.

"I'm not supposed to leave my post," said the guard.

"Really? That order's been rescinded. You're going. This is a matter of life and death."

The look on Vladic's face was enough for the guard. "Yes sir," he said.

The dean was home, and after hearing Vladic tell him that the information was essential to the investigation of the terrorist attacks, he accompanied the two men back to the administration building. As expected there was no Gauss listed, but he did obtain Alan Kanter's home address. "We may be back in an hour with another name to look up, so don't leave your house, sir."

As hoped for, Alan Kanter was home. When he saw the official looking men at his door he was frightened. What woman is after me, he thought? So he was relieved, but confused to discover the purpose of the visit was to learn about Gauss. "Sure, I know him, he said. What's this all about?"

"We just need your answer to what's his name," said an impatient Vladic.

Alan knew instantly that these men would brook not stalling. "His name is Ben Marzan."

"Where does he live?"

"He's from Madison Wisconsin, but I don't know his address there. Most students are home now during this short holday."

Besides the fact that Ben was "quiet and strange and acted like his mind was other places and he's a math genius," Alan had no other information to share.

Vladic said, "Thanks, Alan. This visit never took place. You get my drift? You tell anyone and you're in deep shit, son."

"Uhh, yes, sir," said a wide-eyed Alan.

Vladic and Galinski drove back to the dean's house and returned with him to the administrative building. The dean retrieved Ben's address and phone number in Madison.

Back in Vladic's car, Galinski said, "What kind of a name is Marzan?"

"Beats the hell out of me, but we're going to find out when we get to Madison."

Vladic called the home of the only Marzan in Madison. A woman answered. "Hello. Is Ben there?" Vladic asked.

"Yes, who's calling please?"

"A school friend," and then he hung up. "She'll think we got cut off. Let's get in my car and go."

"We're not exactly going by the book, you know," said Galinski.

"Fuck the book! These are times that necessitate shortcuts."

"You're right."

"We got the warning from our Islamic TV friend. What do you think he means?" asked Vladic.

"At the station everyone assumes he meant nuclear."

"You got that right. It's that until proven otherwise. We don't have any time to lose. If this guy, Ben, is involved with what happened in Chicago, the fact that he's in Madison now could mean that they're finished seeding Chicago," said Vladic.

"That's a good thought, because the number of new cases is levelling off. Or he could be in Madison seeding the city there."

"Let's hope not."

CHAPTER 37

Madison, Wisconsin:

They arrived at Ben's home and rang the front door bell. Lois Marzan answered the door and looked worried over the sudden appearance of the two strange men. "Yes, what can I do for you?" she asked.

Vladic, in his usual impatient style held up his identification and said, "This is my name and my FBI number, Ma'am, we have to talk to Ben Marzan alone."

"But, why. Why do you want to talk to him," she stammered nervously.

"We need to speak with him in private ma'am. Are you his mother?"

"Yes I am," she said tremulously.

"Please get him, ma'am."

"He's studying downstairs."

"Thank you, ma'am. Tell him we want to talk to him, and you can either bring him up here or we'll go down to him. Either way, we need to talk to him alone."

"But why, what did he do?"

"We need to see him, Ms. Marzan."

Lois, seeing the seething fury on Vladic's face, said nothing, but she had a sudden sinking, hollow feeling in her chest. Oh my God, she thought. The Imam! No, it couldn't be.

She walked in a daze to the doorway leading down to the lower level. She called down, "Ben, there's some men who want to talk to you. They're coming down."

"What do they want?" he said.

At that point Vladic had made his appearance downstairs followed by Galinski. "Are you Ben Marzan?" asked Vladic.

"Uhh, yes. Who are you?"

I'm agent Vladic of the F.B.I. and this is Detective Galinski of the Chicago police." They both flashed their identification.

"What do you want?" asked Ben as he stood up from his chair.

"We want to ask you some questions. Please sit down."

"What about?"

"Before the attack on Chicago, were you taking the medicine Cipro?" asked Vladic.

"Uh, no, I wasn't."

"We have a doctor who saw Cipro fall out of your wallet."

At first, Ben didn't understand. Then he remembered. "Oh, that was in Maloney's on Rush Street. That wasn't Cipro. Those were some cold pills."

"The doctor was sure they were Cipro."

"They were cold pills, I tell you. She was at the next table. I remember. I don't think she was close enough to get a good look," said Ben gaining confidence.

"Where did you get those cold pills?"

"At the drug store."

How'd you pay for them? Did you pay cash or use a credit card."

Ben thought quickly. "Cash." He said forcefully.

Both Vladic and Galinski realized that this clue now would lead to a dead end. There was no way they would be able to prove that it was Cipro for sure. And at this time everyone in chicago was taking the medicine to protect themselves. Also, over the counter cold medicine, if that's what it was, purchased in a drug store for cash could not be traced to an individual. Vladic decided to change the line of questioning.

"Tell me about the name Marzan. What's the nationality?"

Ben realized he would have to tell the truth here because they could easily find out. "Marzan is my father's name. He was born in Pakistan, but he's been here for about twenty-five years, I think."

Galinski and Vladic glanced at each other. Vladic continued the questioning. "Is your mother from Pakistan too?"

"No, she was born here in Madison, and her family has been in the United States for six generations she tells me."

"Where were you born?"

"Madison."

"What is your religious belief?"

"I bet I don't have to answer a question like that, but I will. We all go to the Al Hamdi Mosque, here in Madison. My father is very religious."

"What does your father do?"

"Professor of mathematics at the University of Wisconsin here in Madison."

"How come they call you Gauss?"

Ben realized they probably found this out from the same lady doctor at Maloney's. He said, "My friends think I'm pretty good in math, I guess."

"How old are you, Ben?"

"Nineteen."

"You're a freshman, right?"

Ben nodded yes.

"Where did you go to high school?"

"Here at Madison South."

"When did you graduate?"

"About two years ago."

"How come you're only a freshman two years later."

Another question that could easily be checked, thought Ben. "Uh, I went to another school for a year."

"What kind of school?"

"Well, uh, a religious school."

"At the mosque here?"

"Not this mosque."

"Where, Ben?"

"In Pakistan."

"Pakistan? You spent a year there, did you? What did you learn?"

"Islam, all about Islam. My father thought I needed that before I went to college and started on my career. It was great."

"Who taught you there, Ben?"

"The Imam."

"Does he have a name."

"I only know him by Imam."

"Where was this?"

"Al Bakr mosque in Peshawar."

"What did you learn there."

"It was all about the Koran. I learned all the rules. I learned how to live a good life."

"Did you learn about Holy War?" asked Vladic without hesitation.

Instantly Ben shook his head and responded with creased brow and tight lips, "No, sir. Is that what this is about? Are you accusing me of being involved with what's happening in the country?"

"Just following up on every lead. That's our job, Ben. Don't you think we should be doing our job?"

"Uh, yes sir, yes I do."

Realizing that there would be no further pertinent information gleamed from this obviously sharp kid, and having enough current info to keep a team of agents busy for a week, Vladic said, "Okay, Ben. That's fine. We don't have any more questions. You've been cooperative. We appreciate it."

"I hope you catch those people," said Ben relieved now that he had gotten these men off the track. After all, he had an imporetant job to do that could not brook disruption. It was too important for the United States of America.

Driving back to Chicago, Vladic asked Galinski, "What do you think?"

"We don't have much. It's his word against my daughter's about whether those pills were Cipros, but I believe my daughter."

"Yeah, that's right. The kid made a good point about your daughter being at the next table, and not being able to see very well from that distance, but going to Pakistan— brother, that was a bombshell."

"What do we do now?" asked Galinski

"We follow up. This is all we've got. Whoever did this job left no clues. I'll have the Madison office of the FBI put a tail on Ben twenty-four hours a day, and when he gets back to Chicago we'll do the same. We'll have the phone tapped at the Madison home and Ben's room at the dormitory. All incoming mail to Ben in his dormitory and his Madison home will be intercepted. As soon as I get back to the Chicago office, I'll call Washington and put them on the trail of this Imam. Who the hell is he? What does he teach? Is he developing martyrs? I don't know how they'll find out, because dealing with Pakistani intelligence could get right back to him. That'll be up to Washington. We've got to explore all leads. If we're heading for a nuclear explosion, we're in deep shit. We could lose hundreds of thousands or millions. The economy of the country could grind to a halt. Every American citizen is now a member of the U.S. military."

CHAPTER 38

Assessment:

Steve viewed with satisfaction the devestation they had caused throughout the city. Many areas of the rest of the country had their outbreaks of smallpox and anthrax as well, but once it became clear that Chicago was the epicenter, the rest of the nation put strict quarantine measures in place and promptly treated all contacts. This had the effect of minimizing the spread.

After approximately six weeks, Steve read that the number of new case reports was falling. The operation's intent had succeeded, and the city began to lift restrictions. The medical community, including retired doctors and nurses and medical and nursing students, had been drafted for immunization duties. Small pox vaccination was given to four million people. Anthrax immunization was disseminated to all contacts. The city was becoming sanitized. The schools were starting to open. There were at least 2,000 deaths to this point. Any citizen who was nonchalant about the terror threat before, now realized that they were in a full-blown World War. There were calls for complete mobilization and the return of the military draft. But there were still those who wanted to disband the military. The country rallied behind their president for the most part, but some still blamed him, called him the world's greatest terrorist and called for his impeachment.

Steve knew that the main concern of the American government now was terrorism's new threat. The thoughts were that it could be nuclear, but there was no intelligence to confirm that fear. Only Steve knew the identification of the cargo that had been brought in to the United States through the Port of Miami. Even the Florida Holy Warriors had not been told what it was they helped smuggle into the country. Besides Steve, the only ones in the know were terrorism's higher ups including the Imam who was given responsibility to implement the program. It was now up to Steve to set the wheels in motion. The deadline for the threat imposed by international terrorism was approaching.

In washington the FBI and CIA cooperated to investigate the Imam whose part in this conspiracy was becoming known. It was found that the Imam, who had trained Ben in the year before Ben started school had been born into a family of religious scholars, and he began his religious training as a very young child. It soon became apparent that he would follow in his grandfather's footsteps as a recognized prodigy who would master the Koran before his teen years, and hold his own in debates with the religious masters. Early on he went to the holy city of Oom in central Iran to study with the masters, and followed that with a trip to Najaf in Iraq where he studied as well. Some of the Grand Masters with whom he worked believed in keeping out of political movements, and others disagreed with that approach, insisting that politics and religion were inseperable. In the latter philosophy, the only true path to world harmony was the religious path with the world under the control of a religious Isamic ruler.

The Imam chose the latter approach, and this brought him into contact with Al-Qaeda. From this point on he led a double life. To the outside world he was a religious scholar who taught Koran and peace. Unbeknownst to all of his followers and the American investigators, he became the principle instructor on Holy War for Al-Qaeda and those similar type conspirators to follow. This was taught only in private sessions with those that he felt were amenable and pliable enough to absorb such instruction and be influenced by its teachings. Over the years he had become terrorism's principle promoter and cultivator of Holy Martyrs. They were a vital component to carry the struggle forward and Islamize the world. He developed an uncanny ability to identify potential recruits, and when Ben Marzan came to his school for instruction, he recognized his precarious mental state, his open and pliable mind, renamed him Yusuf, and placed him on his private instruction list.

The CIA and FBI agents in Pakistan only learned of the Imam's school that taught the principles of the Koran. His second life remained a secret only to him and the Imams of terrorist groups and his private instructees, all of whom had been assigned to suicide operations in different parts of the world. The one involving Ben was so important, that even Ben was not to learn about it until after the first part of his task would be completed.

After several more weeks had passed, and the life of the wounded city was approaching normal, Steve needed to meet with his three fellow Trojan Horses, so he wrote them all a letter and mailed it to their places of residence. He used a post office far from his Addison Street address with a woman's name as sender. Ben received the letter at the dormitory. The message was—meet me at North Side Athletic Club 6 in the evening, Saturday. Sign in for the one day trial so you can get in. Use a fake name and address. S. To Jenny he wrote and told her to be there at 7. To Joe, 8 o'clock.

What Ben didn't know was that the letter had been intercepted and read by Galinski and Vladic who said, "I don't know who the hell this S is, but you and I will be there, in disguise, at 5:30. We'll get in a little exercise and keep our eyes peeled for Ben. We'll watch his every move. I'll have another man stationed in the parking lot, so that we can all follow this S to wherever the hell he goes after the meeting. I think this is important, because S. wrote him an incognito note and told him to sign in with a fake name. This is hot, Galinski. I think your daughter has put us on to the perps."

"I'm beginning to agree with you," said Galinski

Galinski and Vladic arrived at the club, one disquised with fake mustache, and the other with a beard and hair piece. They signed in with fake names and addresses for the one day trial to see "if we like the place." Galinski took up a position near the entrance so he could keep a lookout for Ben.

At 6:00 sharp Ben walked in the club, signed in at the desk, and went back to the exercise equipment with Galinski following him. One man left his machine, approached Ben, and shook his hand. Then they went in to the bar and sat down at one of the tables. That has to be S thought Galinski. He signaled Vladic and they followed them into the bar.

CHAPTER 39

Trojan Horses meet:

"Good work, Ben," said Steve. "We're doing great. You should be proud of what you've accomplished."

"Thanks, Steve. I did what I was told to do. I'm sure the Imam is happy, too."

"I can assure you he is. How's school, Ben?"

"It's good. The math keeps getting harder. It's a challenge. I couldn't work one problem once, and the teacher told me it was a trick problem. It had no answer, and I fell into the trap."

Steve noted Ben's facial expression turn to sadness, and he said, "Did that bother you, Ben?"

"Oh yeah! I hate it when I can't work it out."

"Did you go home to Madison when school was closed, Ben?"

"Yeah I did."

"How are your folks, Ben?"

"They're good, thanks."

"Be glad, Ben because these operations, like the one we just carried out, will bring Allah to the whole world. It's just a matter of time. If it takes one year or one hundred years, it doesn't matter, and people like us will be responsible for all the good that will come. Everytime I think about that I feel proud."

Ben nodded.

"We're not finished here yet," said Steve.

"We're not?"

"No, not yet. We have one more thing to do. And I tell you, Ben, the Imam has said that you should be the one to carry it out. I mentioned that before, you remember. He must think the world of you, Ben. Very few of us are ever given that honor."

Ben sat up straight. His stared at Steve with anticipation in his eyes. He sipped his coke and said, "I know. That's what you told me. What is it? What does the Imam want me to do?" he asked innocently although he felt sure he already knew.

"Ben, I wish I could tell you, but I haven't been told yet," lied Steve. "All I know is that I received information from the Imam, and he said that a wonderful operation is being planned, and it will bring glory to the one who carries it out. He wants you, Ben. Think on that, it's you he wants!"

Ben with wide opened eyes and an almost hypnotic stare asked, "When will I know?"

"The only thing the Imam said was that I would get more information soon, and just be patient. As soon as I have the word I'll send you another letter and we'll meet again."

Ben, glowing in the praise from the Imam, was distracted. He would not tell Steve about the agents that came to his house in Wisconsin and questioned him when he thought, they were just following up a stupid coincidence with the Cipros when they fell out of my wallet, and that lady doctor saw them. It was her word against his, and nothing could be proven, plus since he hadn't heard a thing from the agents for a couple of weeks, he was in the clear. Ben needed to know what this important job was, although he was confident he knew what it was—but kept the quizical look on his face.

"You could go now, Ben. I'll be in touch, said Steve."

"Okay, thanks, Steve," answered Ben.

Steve went back to his exercise machines. Precisely at 7:00, a stunning lady approached him. Vladic and Galinski's eyes opened widely, and they looked at each other with raised eyebrows. This time they did not follow them into the bar, but kept a close look at the entrance and exit from the bar so as to see when the lady would leave. Vladic realized that the man he stationed out in the parking lot was told that he would be following a male, so he went out and told him that he was to follow a woman instead, and he would identify her to him at the time she left.

"Jenny, I speak as one who is perfectly assimilated, you are hot, babe," said Steve.

"Blimey, honey, you can sure butter up a gal."

"You did a great job, Jenny. We have the infidels on the run."

"It was my pleasure, Steve. I wish we could do more."

"We'll all have more chances, believe me. But now we lay low for a while after a job well done."

"Okay, Steve, I waited a long time for this job. I hope I won't have to wait long for the next one. That's why I stayed in this damn country, you know."

"You'll hear from me within the next month. I'll contact you with instructions."

"By mail?"

"That's right, but it won't be about the next job."

It won't? What'll it be about, Steve," said Jenny, her interest piqued.

"I'll be telling you when to get out of town. Only, Jenny, it'll be a permanent relocation, so trim down your belongings. You'll head West."

"Why West?"

"I can't tell you, but I'll be leaving too. We'll all go to Los Angeles. We'll have plenty of money to live there."

"How will we get in touch with each other?"

"We'll meet. My letter will tell you where and when."

"Okay, Steve. I look forward to further plans, as long as it involves killing infidels."

Jenny left the bar. She didn't know that Vladic had her under observation while he was instructing the driver in the parking lot. When Jenny drove off, the tail was on.

To Vladic and Galinski's surprise, S still remained in the gym. So they continued their surveillance of the bar. They watched as a man walked in, shook hands with S, and together they went into the bar.

"I don't know how many are going to meet this S guy, but if this is the last one, and they both leave together, I'll follow S and you follow the new fellow. In the meantime I'll get another man here just in case more are coming," said Vladic.

"Good thinking," said Galinski.

"We've got to get names and addresses and phone numbers of all these bastards," said Vladic. We'll be on them like flys on honey."

Steve and Joe talked for about ten minutes. Joe was given the same information that Jenny received. Then they left the gym together, and Vladic and Galinski followed them out. Galinski followed Joe's car, and Vladic followed S. By the next morning they would have names, home addresses, phone numbers, social security numbers and places of employment. The four were put under surveillance twenty-four hours per day.

CHAPTER 40

The gauntlet is laid down:

Amanda was not told that her clue had led to the identification of important persons of interest. She forgot about it in the intensity of all her work. The worst of the biological assault was over, and the volume of patients visiting the Emergency Department had receded. Now that medical personnel were alert to the possibility of smallpox and anthrax, the operative words were 'it's smallpox or anthrax until proven otherwise.' Rapid identification techniques became part of the ED procedure. Patients also had the same fears, and if they fell ill they worried about the twin curses before any other consideration. But there was hope for the future, as daily reductions in patient volume offered relief for beleaguered medical personnel and patient alike.

In the meantime, several weeks had passed from the time of the first threat from the terrorist enemy. The airways were filled with discussions and recommendations about what the United States should do about the coming threat, which everyone assumed was nuclear. In the meantime, the government had been speaking with allies around the world with nuclear bomb capability. The purpose was to develop a unified front. The president of the United States put together a nuclear coalition that included Great Britain, France, Russia and India. The Chinese viewed the threat as an idle one. The Pakistan governmnt urged the terrorist groups not to throw the world into nuclear oblivion, but they were not supported by an element of their people sympathetic to this ideology. Israel completed all plans to take out Iran's burgeoning nuclear program.

The advice from American citizens ranged from 'nuke 'em now' to prayer. So everyone awaited word from the American president.

When it came, there wasn't a TV or radio around the world that wasn't turned on. "Citizens of the world, the United States of America has been the victim of a dastardly biological attack involving anthrax and smallpox that has caused billions of dollars of economic damage, and killed thousands of our innocent citizens. The perpetrators of this outrage are stateless murderers who care not whether they expand the current World War into one that will make I and II combined, pale by comparison. They risk this outcome because they believe that they will inherit the earth and instill their poisonous philosphy on the survivors. They target civilians of all ages and nationalities, including those of their own religion, a religion that they have distorted to suit their murderous philosophy.

"Let our enemies know that we are not sitting by waiting for them to destroy us. We have put together a coalition that will answer with power if there is one more attack on one of our countries. In the name of our citizenry, on this I swear."

That was it. Eighty seconds and done. The world stood numb. Comments in the United States ranged from 'thank God, another Churchill has finally arisen, to murderer-terrorist!'

Many in the Muslim world protested and took to the streets, killing many of their own in the riots that ensued. Other Muslims, at the risk of their own lives, pleaded with terrorism to withdraw their threat. The president of Pakistan received a tenfold increase in death threats. The American engendered coalition came out in support of the president. The world stood on the brink of disaster.

Meanwhile, authorities in the United States strategized on how to abort the coming attack on Chicago.

CHAPTER 41

Abel Gondorf, Homeland Security:

The next morning, before Amanda went to work, Vladic and Galinski appeared at her door. "What are you doing here so early in the morning, dad? Then with terror in her voice she said, "Is mom okay?"

"Mom's fine, Don't worry. This is FBI agent Vladic, Amanda. Where working together on the bio-warfare case."

Confused and still amazed by the visit from her dad, she said, "Pleased to meet you, sir." Then she turned to Detective Galinski and said, "What's this all about, dad?"

"In two hours we're leaving for Washington D.C. You need to come with us, Amanda."

A stunned Amanda could only say, "But why? What's this all about?"

Vladic answered, "You've given us the principle lead in solving the biowarfare attack, and people in Washington want you to be at a meeting they're holding today."

Gauss, thought Amanda—Gauss—it was real. He was behind this. Oh my God. She looked at her father and with wide-opened eyes and mouth, nodded her head. She was speechless.

Galinski said, "Call the hospital and tell them you can't be there on an urgent matter. Leave it to me to follow up with your boss. I'll take care of it. No one must know where you are going today."

"What can I tell them, dad?" said a worried Amanda.

"Just that an urgent matter makes it impossible to be there. We'll cover for you later. Trust us, Amanda. We can't give them the true reason. We're in a hurry. Every second counts."

Vladic, Galinski and a very surprised Amanda were driven to O'Hare field where a waiting private jet flew them to Washington D.C. They arrived in two hours and met in the office of Homeland Security in a large rectangular shaped office with a fourteen seat conference table. Representatives of the organization as well as members of the FBI and CIA were present. At the head of the table sat the director of the office of Homeland Security, a former New York District Attorney named Abel Gondorf, a tall, thin and balding man with a loud and firm deep voice. "Doctor Galinski, first I want to thank you on behalf of our country for giving us our only firm lead in this horrible attack."

A shy and overwhemed Amanda stammered, "Uhh…Thank you, sir."

"Doctor, this meeting never took place, you understand."

"I understand, sir."

"We won't keep you long. Tell us about this young man, this Gauss fellow—Ben Marzan."

Amanda reported the story of how they met at Maloneys.

"I know this may be asking a lot from you after meeting Marzan only for a few minutes, but as a physician do you have any medical impression of this young man."

"Well, yes I do. He was there with three other older students. I would say the others looked like they were seniors, and the young man looked like a freshman. He clearly appeared uncomfortable sitting there with the older boys. He looked out of place. I noted that his left leg was shaking."

"How do you mean, doctor?

"Let me show you." Amanda went to a chair along the wall, sat down and demonstrated what Ben had done.

"Were you able to get any impression of his mental state?"

"If I had to guess after a five minute observation, I would say he was insecure and anxious, maybe depressed, perhaps. It was as if he didn't want to be there. These young men were college boys, and the spokesman made a pass at us. That's the simplest way I can put it. I discouraged them and ended any ideas they may have had with a one line joke. Everyone thought what I said was funny and laughed out loud, but not the young guy. He just stared into space. It was as if he was somewhere else. My one-liner worked though, and they left the premises."

"What about the pills that fell out of his wallet?"

"They were Ciprofloxacin tablets."

"Are you certain?"

"I am certain. There is no doubt. They were rectangular shaped with curved ends, and they were white. They were the 500 milligram tablet."

I'm told this was right before the attack on the city."

"Yes sir, that's correct."

"What is Cipro used for, doctor?"

"Principally urinary tract infections, and of course now anthrax, so he might have been using it for a urinary infection, but in a young man that is not common. Anyhow, with the anthrax attack, I couldn't help thinking about the connection and the fact he could have been using it for anthrax propylaxis."

"I see, doctor. That may turn out to be one of the most important hunches in our brief history. Your serendipity may prevent the coming attack. We're grateful for your service and may God bless you. Does anyone here have any other questions?"

None forthcoming, Gondorf said, "Okay then. Doctor, thank you for coming. I wanted to meet and talk to you and thank you on behalf of the American people. If this astute observation of yours leads to the disruption of the terrorist's plot against our country, we will all owe you an incalculable debt of gratitude. Also, doctor, I want to thank you for your selfless work for the victims of this dastardly attack. The country owes you, and the entire medical profession, the highest accolades for what you all have done."

"Thank you, sir."

Detective Galinski held back his tears of pride. Then he said, "She caught smallpox, sir, but thank God it was only a mild case."

Gondorf looked at Amanda, a look of concern on his face. "I didn't know that, doctor. Thank God is right."

"I was lucky. I got the vaccination at the right time," said Amanda.

Gondorf answered quietly, "Doctor, we're all grateful for your good fortune. The entire country and the president of the United States thanks you. Now, we'll drive you to the airport and get you back to your work."

She hugged her father and left. Galinski could not hold back his tears.

After Amanda left, Gondorf said, "Mr. Vladic, let's hear your report."

"Yes. sir. On the strength of Dr. Galinski's clue, we interviewed the suspect, Ben Marzan. I'm sure we left him with a feeling that he answered all the questions to our satisfaction, and so we haven't seen him again. We want him to think that we've gotten off the trail because he satisfied us that he's got nothing to do with what happened in Chicago. We hope that this has made him feel he's home free, and doesn't have to worry about us. But, we've got him under twenty-four hour surveillance, and this led us to the other three suspects that we've identified. We've got a large team of men and women keeping all four of them on twenty-four hour surveillance. I have to think that these are the people who seeded the city with the bugs. How they got hold of them, and where they came from I have no idea."

"What about the year that Marzan spent in Pakistan?"

"The Imam who taught him has a reputation as a brilliant cleric. We have no evidence that he's involved with Al-Qaeda, Isis, or any other terrorist group. But I have to wonder, because this kid, Ben, sure didn't come up with this stuff all on his own."

"It's all pretty suspicious isn't it?" asked Gondorf.

"Yes, for sure, answered Vladic."

"Detective Galinski, do you have anything to add?"

"Only that I'm convinced these are the people involved. The bad news is they're all American citizens. We checked their background, and three of them weren't born here. One in Lebanon, one in Saudi Arabia and one in Palestine. The Saudi Arabian is the one in charge. He's the one who met with all three at the health club. Between the FBI and our Chicago police, they'll never get out of our sight. That I can guarantee. They are all Trojan Horses in our midst"

"That's an appropriate statement, detective. We've been invaded. Thank you, sir. Agent Vladic, we've got about a month to go before their threat to attack us again. What do you recommend?" asked Gondorf.

"First, we don't know for certain, but, I'm pretty sure it's safe to make the assumption, from the nature of the threat, that they want to explode a nuclear bomb. If that's true it means it's already here and hidden someplace in Chicago, or else they're bringing it in soon. If they are bringing it in, the question is how? It has to be either by boat through one of many ports, or by plane. Or even the Mexican border or the Canadian border. How do we tighten all that up? How do we check everything that comes in? It would be an impossible task…"

Gondorf interrupted."Nevertheless, we have to do it. Impossible is a word we can not afford to use."

"Right, sir."

Galinski added, "I believe the bomb is already in place."

Vladic added, "Yes, I agree, otherwise why would they make such a definite threat?"

"Let's think a minute," said Gondorf. The borders will have to be my responsibility. We'll have to boost those up to the greatest extent possible. We may have to call out the National Guard. I'll deal with that. I'll speak with the Pentagon about this today. The FBI, CIA, and the police will deal with the assumption that the bomb is already here. Vladic, what do you propose?"

"We've discussed two options, sir. First option: we'll continue to tail the suspects and hope that they will lead us to the bomb. If I were them, I would store it in a storage bin until I was ready to use it. Second option: we've got enough on them to put them all away now, so we could arrest them all and keep it quiet from the press. We'd lock them up, and throw away the key. Then they couldn't carry out the attack. That option has risks, because I'm sure the terrorist higher-ups have have already ordered the attack, and if they can't get hold of their people in Chicago, he could assign some others to the task, and there's the possibility we will never be able to identify them."

"So it sounds like you're in favor of the first option," said Gondorf.

"Yes sir. Galinski and I have been through this many times. Option number one is the safest bet in our opinion. But, in the meantime, we're going to go to every storage facility in Chicago and within fifty miles of the city. We've got pictures of all the suspects. We plan to ask every storage boss if they recognize anyone of the four."

"Won't that arouse suspicion?" asked Gondorf.

"We plan to tell them we're looking for stolen goods."

Gondorf nodded his head. "Okay, let's get to work."

CHAPTER 42

Message number two:

"We have had no response, nor do we see any movement of infidel troops from Holy Muslim lands. We will extend our warning to another two weeks, and if in that time there has been no change, we will unleash our retribibution as promised." That was the end of the message. It was delivered via audiotape.

The president's brief address was answered in kind, short and to the point. The world embarked upon a diplomatic flurry such as had not been seen since 1914 and 1939. The diplomacy was led by the European powers who began to realize that they were on the threshold of a nuclear holocaust. The diplomatic activity was one-sided however, as terrorism's side was stateless, and could not be reached for comment.

Many Chicagoans were beginning to evacuate the city. Those that could not leave, sent their children to relatives out of state. The psychological impact of the war of words was overwhelming. Mental health problems were now the most commom reason for a visit to a physician's office or hospital emergency room.

"What's going to happen, dad?" asked Amanda one Friday evening during dinner at her parent's house. A fellow officer associate of Galinski's, named Jim Dunlap was also present. Amanda was introduced.

"Thanks to you, Amanda we're hot on the trail of four suspects. We'll stop them. We have to," said Galinski.

"Four?" said a surprised Amanda. "Who besides the young guy taking Cipro?"

Galinski realized he spoke too soon. "Sorry, Amanda, I slipped. It's not something I can talk about."

"But why? You know I can keep a confidence."

"I know that, but we're following them twenty-four hours a day. As far as we know they have no idea we're doing this. But they could know if your suspect, Ben, told his superior that we interrogated him. Ben knows that you were the one who fingered him, so the less you know the better. We have reason to believe that Ben didn't say anything, because if he did, he would be kept out of the loop, and so far we don't think that has happened."

"How do you know?"

"First of all we've never gone back to ask Ben any more questions. We hope he'll get the idea that we couldn't find anything on him, so he's in the clear. Also there's been no change in any of their behaviors. There's nothing suspicious as best as we can tell. But I'm not taking any chances as far as you're concerned."

"What do you mean, dad?"

"I mean that you're being watched day and night."

A startled Amanda shook her head. "But why?"

"In case this prime suspect, Ben, told his superiors about our interrogation, they may be interested in you, Amanda. I worry."

"You're having me followed?"

"Yes, every minute."

"But who?"

"He's right here at the table."

"Jim?"

"Yes, Jim. You need to know. If you notice anyone else watching you, tell Jim that very second."

"Oh, God, dad, I'm speechless. Jim will be following me whereever I go?"

"That's right, Amanda. Just pretend he's not there. Never mention him to anyone."

The next day, Galinski met Vladic at his office. "We've come up against a dead end on the renter of the storage bin, if that's what was rented," said Vladic.

"It still doesn't mean it isn't there. If I were them I would disguise myself when I rented," said Galinski. "Maybe we should have all storage bins opened that have been rented in the last three months."

"We've thought of that too. We also thought of monitoring for radiation, but we've been told that if packaged right the radiation would not be detectable." We're going to do it all. We can't afford to leave any possibility unchecked."

CHAPTER 43

Ben beakdown?

Ben had immersed himself into his mathematics, but he again experienced a frightening development: He was having increasing difficulty in solving problems. This difficulty was not a failure to understand the mathematical concept involved, but it was more a difficulty in being able to concentrate on the task. He found his mind wandering, and he was having sudden fears that would increase his breathing and pulse rate. There were other times when a math problem was so engrossing that he was able to concentrate. When he was succesful in solving a problem he would find himself calmer and more relaxed, but when a problem did not lend itself to a solution, all his nervous symptoms would return. I must control this he thought, the job I have to do is too important.

It became apparent to Professor Jamison that when Ben came to him with a problem that he could not solve, all was not well with his most brilliant student. Jamison noticed a mask-like, melancholic appearing expression on Ben's face as he described the difficulty he was having. He spoke in a monotone when he reached the point where he failed to comprehend the problem, and when he did understand, his facial expression and voice changed for the better. These were such extreme opposites, and they happened so rapidly to Ben, that Jamison realized that there could be something wrong with Ben, and he expressed concern.

"Ben, are you alright? Is anything bothering you?"

"I'm okay. It's just that a tough problem seems to get to me."

"Do you realize how far ahead of every other undergraduate you are?"

"Uh, I don't think of things like that."

"Well you are way ahead. Most students have math problems in the first grade. Some in second, some in third and up the line. I think maybe everything has been so easy for you up to this point, that you're beginning to feel the frustration that most people feel long before this point. Now the real challenge starts, Ben. Are you going to give up because you're finding it a little difficult? I don't think so. Now is when the challenge starts. Now is when we separate the men from the boys. Now you decide. Will you go on and accept the challenge, or will you change your major now?"

"Change my major? Never, professor, never!"

"Fine then. Let's get back to work."

"Yes, sir," he answered. Then he thought, what I have to do is too important. Perhaps I should stay away from math for a short while.

CHAPTER 44

More evidence:

Later when Ben returned to his dormitory room there was a letter in his mailbox. It had no return address. He opened it and saw a hand written printed two sentences: B. I'll pick you up at McDonald's after you finish work Monday. We'll go for a ride. S.

That's all there was to it. Instructions from Steve. Maybe now I'll find out for certain what it was that Steve was talking about when we met last, thought Ben.

Vladic and Galinski intercepted the letter. "We've got to know what this conversation is about," said Vladic.

"I agree," said Galinski. We can wire Ben's car while he's in class, and Steve's car while he's working. Steve will probably drive his car, but we can't take the chance on not wiring Ben's."

"Right. We'll have to do it Friday morning," said Vladic. I'll get our electronic experts on the job, stat."

The best men in the country were assigned the task. The most inconspicuous and modern electronic wizardry was implanted in both cars.

Steve showed up at McDonald's at nine. Ben was at the front counter. Steve walked up to the counter. "I'll have a small order of french fries and a small drink, please," he said.

Ben gave Steve his order. Steve paid and whipered to Ben, "I'll meet you outside when I see you leave."

There were men stationed to follow them when they left, and Vladic and Galinski were at the listening post in another car to pick up and record the conversation.

Ben and Steve got into Steve's car and headed west on Simpson Street.

"How are you, Ben?" asked Steve.

"I'm okay."

"Are you sure, Ben?"

"Yeah, I'm sure."

"How's the math, Ben?"

"It gets tougher."

"I believe that. I was never very good at math. I didn't have to go much past calculus, and that was enough for me," said Steve.

Steve noted Ben fidgeting in the front seat. Ben's leg was shaking. "It's official, Ben. The Imam wants you for the job."

"What job?"

"We'll pull it off in about two weeks, but I'm not allowed to tell you yet."

"When will I know?"

"Soon, Ben. I'm trying to figure out why you were given this honor. The Imam says you deserve it. When I think that you've only been involved with the Holy War for about a year and a half, and most of us have been involved for a lot more than that, I keep scratching my head. But my orders are just to follow orders, and when I hear from the Imam, all I say is yes sir. This is a holy martyr operation, Ben. Very few of us are ever given that honor. This is not the usual one like you read about in the newspapers. This is the ultimate of all holy martyr operations in Islamic history. I feel honored to be in your presence, Ben."

Ben said nothing for a short while, his leg still shaking, his eyes fixed straight ahead. "I know what the Imam wants," said Ben calmly.

"I was waiting for you to figure it out. God knows the whole world knows what's about to happen. It's on every TV program, every newspaper and magazine. You will be the world's center of attention. You will be the greatest hero that the Muslim world has ever produced, second only to Muhammed, Ben. You will have the mind of Allah, and you will never have another math problem that confuses you. The mathematical secrets of the universe will be open to your mind."

Ben didn't speak, a look of rapture was on his face as he stared into the unknown.

When Steve reached Skokie Blvd he turned around and drove Ben back to McDonald's. "I'll be in touch with you one more time, Ben."

Ben went to his carr and drove to the dormitory. He had another restless sleep that night.

"That's about all the evidence we need," said Vladic. "These four are it, and Ben is the trigger man. Where the hell is that bomb? We've got a lot of thinking to do."

"We can't be thinking too long; we're runnig out of time," answered Galinski."

CHAPTER 45

Deadline approaches:

Vladic and Galinski reported to Washington about the conversation between Steve and Ben They were told to fly there immediately. From this point forward the decisions would have to be made at the federal level. The director of the CIA and the FBI were also present.

"That was an incredible bit of sleuthing. You've found the perpetrators beyond a doubt," said Gondorf.

"Thank you, sir," said Vladic.

"What are your thoughts now?" asked Gondorf.

Vladic said, "The conversation we taped was very specific, and points to these people as the ones prepared to explode the nuclear bomb, even though they never said so. We know that the youngest one, the freshman student at Northwestern University, Ben Marzan, has been the one picked to deliver the bomb, and according to the boss that was the Imam's decision, and that has to be the Imam that trained the kid."

"I agree." said Gondorf.

"Yes," said Vladic, "but we have another bit of evidence that points to at least one of them, and more than likely all of them as the perpetrators of the biological attack."

"What's that?"

"We entered the house of the leader of the group, Steve, while he was at work. We found smallpox vaccination and anthrax immunization supplies in his refrigerator. We took pictures and left the stuff there so as to not arouse any suspicions."

"You're left open to the charge of manufacturing evidence," said the FBI director.

"I know sir, but there it was for sure. That's all I can tell you. We have movies of our entering the house, and of every move we made in there, including opening the front door, the refrigerator and seeing the evidence."

"All without a search warrant?"

"No sir. We got probable cause from a judge."

"What do you recommend we do as the next step?" asked Gondorf.

"We've still got the same problem. We know the perps, but we don't know where the bomb is. We don't think that any of the four would be able to store the bomb where they work. We don't think they would keep it in their homes, but we can't take a chance so we'll check their homes just like we did the boss' apartment. We're in the process of visiting all the storage facilities to see if anyone recognizes any of the four as having rented a bin. So far, no luck."

Galinski added, "The youngest one, Ben Marzan has been picked for the suicide mission, but the boss didn't give him any details yet. He said he would soon, so I believe we've got to keep on tracking them to find out where the bomb is. I don't see any other option. As we pointed out before, we've got enough to arrest them all now, but if we do, and they don't talk, then the bomb is out there, and someone else could get it and explode it, and we'll be helpless to stop it."

"What do you think, Vladic,"

"Yes sir. I agree. If that's our final orders that's what we'll do, sir."

"Does anyone have any other ideas?"

Hearing none, Gondorf said, "Okay lets do it. Don't let those bastards out of our sites. Vladic, I want a call from you at four o'clock every afternoon on this secure line. For emergencies any time, here's my cell phone number." He handed Vladic two phone numbers written on a note pad. "Try and get a little sleep in shifts," said Gondorf

"Yes, sir."

CHAPTER 46

Assessment:

For one full week an army of police checked storage facilities in and around Chicago. The proprietors were unable to identify any of the four suspects as having rented space within the last three months.

"Either the bomb isn't in any storage bin, or it hasn't entered the country yet," said Vladic.

"Or someone rented a bin more than three months ago," said Galinski.

"I suppose that's possible," said Vladic. "Something as big as the planning for this attack must have been in the works for years. We're dealing with patient people. A century to them is like a year to us. From the last meeting with Ben and Steve we know that this is a suicide mission. That's good news because if they do have a bomb in place, why couldn't they just trigger it by radio signal from a distance? Then we'd be helpless to be able to find it in time."

"If that was the case, then the bomb would have to be right where they want it, sitting there waiting to be triggered," said Vladic. "What do you think would be the target they would choose in the Chicago area?"

"The Loop."

"Yeah, I think you're right. That would be my choice too."

Galinski said, "Then we better check every rental space in every storage bin in and around the Loop. If I were them I would find one closest to the western end of the loop. Then any nuclear bomb that would go off, say one that has a two mile diameter of complete destruction, would take out the whole loop and about a mile of the surrounding area."

All storage bins surrounding the loop were checked. No nuclear device was found. There was no choice. This investigation would go down to the wire. Ben Marzan would have to be followed to his destination when and if he was sent on his mission by Steve. As the deadline approached, a phone message to Ben was intercepted. It was, "Come to my apartment at six o'clock Thursday night."

They had three days to act. The same group of the best FBI electronic experts in the country wired Steve's apartment for sound and video.

CHAPTER 47

Waziristan:

In Waziristan, plans were being made for a celebration. The heirarchy of terrorism and all is divisions theroughout the world, were instructed to show up at a deep mountain cave by noon, Friday. The Imam presided. A feast prepared for a very special occasion of thanks to Allah and for the successful completion of the nuclear attack on Chicago scheduled for Friday 7:00 in the morning was laid out in gastronomic splendor. The 7:00 in the morning time coincided with Waziristan time of 3:00 in the afternoon. They would pray, have a late lunch, watch CNN on television and hear the announcement that the City of Chicago, one of the sin cities in the land of the Great Satan, had been reduced to rubble. Then they would get a report from the Imam as to the progress of his work, and begin further preparations for the continuing conflict.

CHAPTER 48

Final instructions:

Ben arrived at Steve's apartment exactly on time. "How are you, Ben?" asked Steve.

"I'm okay."

These two words, delivered in a quiet monotone, alarmed Steve who noted Ben's mask-like facies. "What are you thinking, Ben?"

Ben smiled. "I'm thinking that I'll never have any more trouble with math. Never, ever again." Ben's eyes opened wide. He placed his elbows on the dining room table, made a fist of his left hand and placed it in his right palm. Then he put both hands in front of his face and stared into them. There was a faint smile on Ben's face.

Steve was alarmed. He had been worried about Ben's vaccilating mental state, so he was anxious that the operation would take place as planned tomorrow.

"I have to give you final instructions, Ben. You've got to know what to do."

Ben turned and looked at Steve, the smile on his face replaced by a frown. He nodded. "Yes, I'm ready."

"Take this key, Ben. Don't lose it."

"What is it for?" asked Ben.

"Parked in front of the apartment you'll see a Toyota minivan. Those are the keys to the car. It has no seats except for the driver and front passenger. So there's plenty of room in the back for some cargo. You'll leave your car here and drive the Toyota to your dormitory tonight. Give me the key to your car so I can drive it away from my apartment."

Ben nodded.

"Tomorrow morning you'll drive to this address. Be there at 6:00. It is a storage facility." Steve handed Ben a sheet of paper with the address written on it. "Here's another key, Ben. It will open up the storage bin number A-6. Inside the bin you will see a large box and a moving cart. You'll put the box on the cart and move it to the back of the Toyota and put it in. It's heavy, but I'm sure you can do it. The box will have a wire protruding out of it. Put the wire side of the box facing the front of the car. Have you got that?"

"Yeah, I got it. The wire faces the front of the car."

Steve reached into a dresser drawer and took out what to Ben looked like a gun with a long wire extending from the upper part of the handle. Ben stared at the device with unchanged expression.

Steve continued, "You attach this wire to the wire protruding from the box. It's a plug in system. You know how to do that, Ben?"

Ben nodded. "Yeah," he said softly as he fingered the wire.

"Then you drive to O'Hare field and park in front of the terminal and pull the trigger. Right here, see? It takes some strength. It's not a hair trigger. We don't want it triggered off going over some bump on the road. We know it will be easy for you, Ben, and then there will be no more math problems."

"God is Great," whispered a slightly smiling Ben with eyes closed.

"Let's go over it all again," said Steve. "There's only one chance to get it right, so it's got to be perfect."

CHAPTER 49

More:

Galinski and Vladic heard every word. "Damn, O'Hare field. We should have figured," said Galinski.

"The only thing I can think of is that the destruction of O'Hare will stop airline traffic throughout most of the country. Plus the area is heavily populated. There must be a million people up there. There are hospitals and plenty of industry," said Vladic.

"Another thing, said Galinski, "with the winds going west to east, the radioactive fall out will blanket most of Chicago. It'll be the end of the city."

Vladic said, "I'm calling Gondorf on his cell." He reached him and described the current developments. They discussed strategy. Gondorf informed the President of the United States.

When Ben left Steve's apartment, Steve called Jenny and Joe. His message was quick and to the point. "Just as we planned, leave for Los Angeles late tonight."

Vladic instructed his men to follow Ben back to his dormitory, and he and Galinski would also follow. He instructed his men to arrest Jenny and Joe and Steve when they left their residences.

The minute Steve and Joe left their front entrance they were apprehended by five armed Federal agents. They surrendered meekly.

When Jenny was told she was under arrest, she didn't hesitate. She reached into her purse, screamed God is Great, pulled out a handgun and shot once, wounding an agent. That single shot was all she managed. Nine bullets tore into her body, head and neck, promptly snuffing out her life.

"Right now, that crazy kid is the most important man on the earth," said Vladic.

"Should we take him now?" asked Galinski.

"We could, but I'm afraid he'll destroy the address Steve gave him. Who knows, if he's a zealot like Jenny, he might swallow the damn thing, or he might be armed and go down fighting. We need him alive. We need to follow him to the bomb. I'm going to assign men to watch his dorm room, and watch the exit and entrance of the dorm, and two men to keep their eyes on the Toyota. When he leaves in the morning, we follow him and apprehend him when he tries to pick up his cargo. None of us are going to sleep tonight. I'll have a fresh team here at five-thirty in the morning."

Ben arrived back at the dormitory and parked the Toyota in the student parking lot. He went to his room and sat down at his desk. Then he took a math book off the shelf, and with his leg shaking, he immersed himself in a linear second-order partial differential equation problem. The light stayed on in his room most of the night.

CHAPTER 50

Waziristan:

At 4:00 in the morning Evanston time, while the light in Ben's room was still on, it was noon in Waziristan, and the Imam had arrived. All the invited for the joyous occasion were present. The greetings were warm and heartfelt. They were dressed in their finest white apparel. They prayed on a beautiful oriental rug, and then sat down to the elaborate meal befitting a great day of homage to Allah, a day when the Great Satan, the United States of America, would understand that their days as the major power on this earth would soon come to an end, swallowed up in a large mushroom cloud.

Ben was still awake, pondering the problem he had chosen and wondering if he could solve it before he left for his mission. If he couldn't, he knew and remembered what Steve had once mentioned recently that after he pulled the trigger on the gun, the solution would become obvious, and he would never again have any difficulty. He smiled. His leg did not stop shaking. His smile remained in place.

It was approaching six in the morning in Evanston, Illinois. Ben had continued working. His first path to a solution revealed an answer close to, but different by one term from the book's answer. Where was the error? Frustrated, he had tried another approach, but when his alarm clock rang at six o'clock, he was not yet finished. The clouds along the ceiling were darker, and the voice told him again that the answer was as easy as the squeeze of a trigger. "Uh-huh," said Ben, "funny." He took the Toyota car key, the storage bin key, the gun-trigger and walked calmly to the car.

CHAPTER 51

Waziristan:

It was 2:00 in the afternoon in Waziristan. The satellite feed was working well and Terrorism's heirarchy were sitting around a twenty-four inch television set watching CNN. There were still scattered cases of smallpox and anthrax that were showing up in Chicago and scattered areas of the country, and they viewed that with smiles, laughs and the recurrent God is Great. American television confined itself to news related to the biological attacks and the threat relating to the next attack, assumed to be nuclear until proven otherwise. There was no news about any progress being made by the Americans. They had an hour before the big news, and the air in the cool cave was electric with satisfaction and anticipation.

CHAPTER 52

The last mile:

As Ben, dressed in shorts and a T shirt, walked to the car at 6:00 A.M., there were a dozen pair of eyes on him. He had the pistol-like apparatus with the extruding wire in his pants pocket. He started the Toyota and drove straight west on Simpson, a street that became Golf Road in the adjacent suburb of Skokie. Golf Road continued through Morton Grove, and Ben drove across Milwaukee Avenue adjacent to the Golf Mill shopping center. Approximately two blocks west of Milwaukee Avenue he turned north into a storage facility. He was followed by Galinski and Vladic and ten other FBI agents and members of the Chicago Police Department in four cars. Ben sought Bin A-6, drove past it, and parked his car approximately twenty yards from it. Then he exited his car with hands in the air, turned around and stared directly at his followers who were speechless as they stared at Ben. Ben waved to them and kept his hands high. There was a smile of releif on his face.

Vladic was the first to dispense with this great surprise related to Ben's action and he spoke loudly and clearly to Ben. "Lie down flat on the ground with your hands outstretched in front of you." Ben nodded his head and complied immediately. The others rushed in and immobilized a cooperative Ben who said calmly, "Thank you, gentlemen."

It would be two weeks before any news would issue forth about Ben Marzan. He was incarcerated, surrounded by police guards and famous psychiatrists, and interrogated at length. It would take a while, but finally a 400 page report would emanate from his interviewers declaring that Ben was stable and psychiatrically normal and had perpetrated an amazing deception on his Muslim "friends" by convincing them that he was prepared to carry out the task of destroying America. But he knew he was incapable of doing so, so he collaborated rather than having one of his other Muslim zealot "friends" assigned to perform the deadly task. In time, Ben received numerous awards and became a national hero. When he finally was declared free of any more interrogations, he was allowed to go to Madison, Wisconsin, where his parents met him and the city organized a parade for the hero who had saved the United States of America from the horrible fate of a nuclear explosion. Those Americans who were lackadaisical about the terrorist threats finally realized the folly of their thoughts. The Imam who had worked with Ben for a year in Pakistan said, "My approach was wrong. I will not make this mistake again!"

CHAPTER 53

Endgame:

"How much time do we have?" asked the Imam in Waziristan.

"About fifteen minutes."

With smiles on their faces and raised arms, they all said, There is no God but Allah." They would have a long wait.

Although the threat against Chicago was over, the news would be released only when the live perpetrators were all safely locked up.

Jenny's body was sent back to relatives in the Gaza strip where she was given a martyr's burial. Her flag-draped casket was accompanied to its final resting place by thousands of masked Hamas members carrying Palestinian flags, Kalasnikoff rifles, grenade launchers and pictures of Jenny and her father.

The Holy Warriors in the cave in Waziristan were silent. They watched the TV anticipating a news flash from CNN announcing the destruction of Chicago. They were sure they would have the pleasure of seeing the mushroom cloud over the city. "I wonder what delayed the attack, they thought. As they watched the unchanging TV screen, their hopes began to fade. They sat in silence, beginning to understand that this precision operation, that had taken many years to put in place, had met a snag. The Imam's moving fingers came to rest under his gown.

Finally at 6:00 in the evening in Waziristan, and 10:00 in the morning in Chicago, the news flash came. It announced that the suspected nuclear threat to Chicago was indeed a nuclear threat. Three of the terrorists were apprehended and one was killed after she drew her gun and wounded an FBI agent. The actual nuclear device was found in a public storage facility in Morton Grove, Illinois, and was being dismantled in an unpopulated desert in New Mexico. The country could rest easy. The threat was over. The perpetratoe voluntarily surrendered and would undergo a prolonged interrogation.

They all greeted the news in silence. They sat staring at the screen, and the silence was broken by the Imam who said, "You have to give credit where credit is due. The Americans are to be congratulated."

"I agree. It has not been our first setback, and it won't be the last. Allah is testing our resolve."

"He is; God is Great."

"God is Great."

"It's time to discuss plan B."

THE END

FOR THOSE WITH A MORE SCIENTIFIC BENT, THE
FOLLOWING APPENDICES MAY BE OF INTEREST.

APPENDIX 1

Anthrax is an infectious disease caused by the bacterium *Bacillus Anthracis*.
These bacteria can be found in cattle, sheep, goats and other plant eating
animals. If human beings are exposed to any of these animals, either by
eating or handling tissue from them, or working with their hides, they
can acquire the illness. Anthrax can occur worldwide, and in the United
States can be acquired from wild livestock, although it is a rare occurrence
in this country.

The anthrax bacteria can turn into a spore (an inactive form), and can
survive in the soil for many decades waiting to activate when exposed to
the proper environmental conditions.

Anthrax can be caught in one of three ways: on the skin (cutaneous
anthrax); by inhaling anthrax spores (inhalation anthrax); and eating
undercooked meat of infected animals (gastrointestinal anthrax).

Anthrax of any type manifests itself about seven days after exposure.

Cutaneous anthrax starts as an itchy bump resembling an insect bite.
In about two days a small blister forms, followed by a painless ulceration
that gradually forms a black center due to necrosis (death) of skin. The
lesion grows, and nearby lymph glands may swell when the spreading
anthrax organism reaches them. The mortality rate of untreated cases is
twenty percent, but if treated with the appropriate antibiotic, deaths are
very rare.

Inhalation anthrax may take up to two months for the spores to
reactivate once they have been inhaled into the lungs. Flu-like symptoms

may progress to fever and breathing difficulty that can lead to respiratory failure and death. Without treatment the disease is fatal.

Gastrointestinal anthrax causes inflammation of the gastrintestinal tract, resulting in appetite loss, nausea and vomiting, abdominal pain, vomiting of blood, diarrhea and fever. If untreated, the illness is up to sixty percent fatal.

Interestingly, anthrax is not passed from person to person.

A vaccine has been developed to prevent anthrax, and is given to people who work with the organism, or who work with animal hides and furs. Military pesonnel, who face the potential of biological warfare, are also vaccinated. The vaccine does not contain live bacteria, but rather it contains a protein ingredient common to all anthrax strains. This allows the body to make antibodies against the disease.t.

To diagnose anthrax one has to identify the organism either from the skin, the blood, or the respiratory secretions. It is also possible to identify specific antibodies by blood testing.

The illness is treated by the antibiotic Ciprofloxacin, with alternative antibiotics—either doxycycline or amoxicillin.

APPENDIX 2

In ancient times, smallpox could decimate a town. It could kill fifty percent of a population as well as scarring many for life. The ancient Chinese were the first to understand that anyone fortunate enough to recover from 'the pox' was immune to a future outbreak of the disease. Even those who had a few 'pox' on their skin were as immune as those who recovered from a full-blown case.

An unknown immunology pioneer in China reasoned that if individuals receive a small amount of material from a dried scab scratched onto the skin, they would be immune to future outbreaks. This turned out to be the case. The problem was that at times the person inoculated with the scab material sometimes developed a severe case and died. However, in spite of the risks of inoculation, the practice traveled to India and then to Turkey and other parts of Europe.

Finally, Edward Jennet of England entered the story. When he was younger, a milkmaid told him that she would never catch smallpox because she had already had the 'cowpox.' This is a viral disease, also called vaccinia, and it produces a mild illness—although at that time no one ever heard of a virus. The disease, localized to the teats of the cow, presents as infectious ulcers. A milkmaid could catch the virus through a cut on the skin of the hands or other parts of her body. In 1980, scientists identified the rodent as a natural reservoir for the virus that causes the majority of cowpox infections.

Smallpox, or variola is also a viral disease. Since universal vaccination, there has not been a case since 1977. It is one of the most contagious diseases known to man and is spread by direct contact. Indirect contact is also a prime method of dissemination. It starts with a fever and after about two days, a rash may occur that looks like measles or scarlet fever. Spots starting as a small pimple known as a papule will follow this red rash. The papule then fills with fluid (vesicle), and if bacteria infect the vesicle, it will fill with pus (pustule). The amount of these skin lesions can vary from a few to thousands, and they may be so numerous as to become confluent. In time, the pustule dries up and forms a scab that will fall off and leave a permanent scar.

Sometimes the toxicity is so intense that death can occur even before the actual smallpox blisters have time to form.

If someone gets sick enough with smallpox, he or she may not have much opportunity to spread the disease by contact. They are flat on their back at home. People with mild cases, especially those previously vaccinated, have a greater tendency to spread the disease, as they are still up-and-about. In addition, the smallpox virus is very hardy and may persist on the clothes of an infected victim for more than a year. Laundries may be the source of outbreaks.

Smallpox is not a problem for us today, although the threat of terrorism has raised its ugly head. Those who wish to do us harm could reintroduce the infection. People never vaccinated could get serious outbreaks. The older amongst previously vaccinated may possibly have less serious outbreaks, but may be the principle spreaders of the disease.

Scientists have saved the virus in four laboratories around the world just in case it should ever be necessary to make vaccine. This could be the source for bio-terrorism if the samples are not well controlled.

After learning about the immunity of the milkmaids, in 1796, Edward Jenner, a country doctor, took pus from a cowpox sore and scraped it in two cuts on the arm of a young boy. Six weeks later, he did the same with smallpox pus. The boy came down with cowpox, but did not get smallpox. He repeated this experiment twenty-three times until he was able to conclude that those who had cowpox were immune to smallpox. The milkmaids were right. 'I had cowpox, so I'll never get smallpox.'

Jenner named his new method 'vaccination' as opposed to the Chinese developed process of inoculation with the actual smallpox pus. Jenner proved that a mild form of a similar disease could somehow provide the body with immunity to a more virulent form. He did this without knowing anything about bacteria, viruses, nonspecific or specific immunity. He just knew it worked. These experiments of Edward Jenner led to the eventual eradication of smallpox 181 years later. Today's environment would not be conducive to such human experimentation, as the medico legal as well as the health risk would be too great.

APPENDIX 3

NUCLEAR ENERGY

In 1930, James Chadwick, a British physicist, confirmed that there was a neutral particle within the nucleus of an atom. He named it the neutron, so named because of its electric neutrality. Except for the predominant form of hydrogen, the nucleus of all other atoms in the universe consists of protons and neutrons.

An atom has a nucleus containing protons (positively charged) and neutrons (no charge). Surrounding this nucleus, and rotating around it—as the earth revolves around the sun—are negatively charged electrons balancing the positive charge of the protons in the nucleus.

A neutron is a particle that has almost the same weight and size as the proton, but since it is electrically neutral, it has no affect on the positive electrical charge of its nuclear neighbor, the proton.

Since opposite charges attract, why does not the electrically negative electron attracted into the positively charged nucleus as it speeds around it? It took the discoverers of quantum mechanics in the earlier part of the twentieth century to explain why the electron did not spiral into the nucleus. The answer: an electron does not give up energy when rotating in a stable orbit, or if an electron is more like a wave, an electron wave fits exactly within the orbit and with this snug fit gives off no energy. Therefore, the energy between the electron and the proton is perfectly balanced (as is the earth rotating around the sun).

If that explains the electron's stability in the atom, how does one explain the fact that in elements that have multiple protons, why do these positive protons not repel each other as like charges are supposed to do? The answer brings to the fore another important concept: A *nuclear force* binds the protons in the nucleus together. As you can imagine, this force is very powerful and important, for without it atoms could not exist and we would all be part of some primordial soup of energy waiting to evolve.

This force, called the *strong nuclear force*, acts only within the nucleus of an atom at a range of only 0.000000000000001 meters (one quadrillionth of a meter), and acts as glue holding the nucleus in one piece. At the tiny range within which it acts, this force has the ability to push protons apart if they come too close, or push them together if they get too far apart. To put it in context, this strong nuclear force is 100,000,000,000,000,000,0 00,000,000,000,000,000,000 (one hundred unodecillion, or 100 billion billion billion billion times greater then the force of gravity. Inside the nucleus the strong nuclear force is also one hundred times stronger than the electromagnetic force (the force between electrically charged particles like the electron and proton), and one million times stronger than the weak force which is a force responsible for radioactive decay (explained later).

In order for the strong nuclear force to work, the protons and neutrons within the nucleus must be very close together, no farther than the diameter of one of the particles. When they are this close, there is an exchange of a particle called a meson, which bounces back and forth between the protons like a ping-pong ball, and this bouncing back and forth keeps the nuclear particles together. If the protons cannot get this close to each other, the strong force does not have the power to keep them together and they will move apart because of the electromagnetic force of repulsion.

The neutrons in the nucleus help to reduce the force of repulsion between protons. Since neutrons have no charge they do not add to any repulsion in the nucleus and they help to keep the protons apart. This enables shielding of a proton somewhat from the repulsive force of other protons. Since the neutrons also participate in the meson exchange, they too are the source of some of the strong force.

With this knowledge, one can understand why it is easier to bombard a nucleus with a neutron than a proton. A neutron will not be repulsed (it has no charge) as it speeds toward a positively charged nucleus and therefore can break the electrostatic repulsion barrier and become incorporated into the nucleus, or otherwise do their nuclear mischief (splitting the atom) so critical for the nuclear era.

Hydrogen has only one proton in the nucleus (no neutron), and one electron rotating around the nucleus.

After hydrogen, the next element is helium. Its most abundant form has two protons and two neutrons and two negatively charged electrons in orbit.

The third element is lithium and its most common form has three protons, three neutrons, and three electrons.

The fourth element is beryllium. It is most common form has four protons, five neutrons, and four electrons.

The fifth element is boron. It has five protons, six neutrons, and five electrons.

The sixth element is carbon. It has six protons, six neutrons, and six electrons.

As we go up the list of the elements, we note that the number of neutrons becomes greater, so that by the time we get to uranium we have an atom consisting of ninety-two protons, and 146 neutrons. These extra neutrons have relevance, as we shall see later.

We've touched upon the strong force that keeps the nucleus together. Such a powerful force means that there is an incredible amount of energy tied up in the nucleus of an atom. To better understand this energy, let us assume that two protons are the size of two single jellybeans. Now let us decide to have one attract the other by bringing them closer together. If we did that, and tried to measure the force and speed of the attraction, it would be the equivalent of two freight trains, each weighing two thousand tons, or four million pounds hurling together at close to the speed of light. Such is the nature of the force tied up in the nucleus of the atom, and this was quantified by Albert Einstein when he developed his famous equation $E=MC^2$ (Energy is equal to mass times the speed of light squared).

To attempt to come to grips with this concept let us go back in time about fifteen billion years to the Big Bang. If we accept the Big Bang concept as explaining the origin of the universe, then we accept the fact that there was an enormous amount of energy virtually concentrated at a point. This energy liberated itself by an explosion that traveled through a developing time and space. As the milliseconds and eons passed, this energy coalesced into the matter of our universe: planets, stars and galaxies. So, is it a surprise that mass is in reality a coalesced form of energy? Mass and energy are two different forms of the same thing. Since some of the energy of the primordial universe has become mass, why could not the mass become energy? Einstein showed us that if we destroy mass we would get back an amount of energy equivalent to the mass lost times the square of the speed of light.

To turn this into meaningful numbers, let us assume that we start with a mass of one gram. A gram is a little more than one thirtieth of an ounce. The speed of light is 186,000 miles per second. Since we are working with a gram of mass, let us turn the 186,000 miles per second into centimeters per second to allow us to stay with the metric system. One hundred eighty-six thousand miles per second works out to thirty billion centimeters per second. Squaring this number, we get nine hundred quintillion centimeters per second or nine hundred million million million centimeters per second (900,000,000,000,000,000,000) depending upon what way of saying it is more meaningful to you.

Now, using Einstein's formula, we get E = one gram times nine hundred million million million centimeters per second. That equals nine hundred million million million ergs. What is an erg? Consider it a measure of energy and suffice it to say that this many ergs is plenty of energy. In fact, it is enough that if you utilized this amount of energy you would win a tug of war contest against sixty five billion horses. Another way of trying to understand it is to say that the one gram of mass would liberate an amount of energy equivalent to burning fifty thousand tons or one hundred billion pounds of coal. Incredible!

Another important point to understand is that the strong nuclear force, which as we discussed, can only make itself felt over tiny distances (one ten million millionth of a centimeter), is in contrast to the electromagnetic force which decreases slowly over distance. This difference is responsible for the occurrence of fission taking place in large nuclei such as uranium. Fission is the splitting of a heavy nucleus into two or more pieces because of the impact of a neutron on a nucleus. Plutonium, uranium, and thorium are the elements capable of splitting in this manner. If this sounds like what you have heard in reference to nuclear bombs or nuclear energy, you are correct.

It is important to understand that in a large nucleus, due to the nature of the strong nuclear force and the fact that each proton or neutron only has a small finite number of such fixed neighbors, a proton or a neutron only feels the force of its close neighbors.

Because of the long range of the electromagnetic force, all protons in the nucleus are influenced by each other. Therefore, the more protons there are, the more the repelling electromagnetic force becomes significant. The result of this is that such large nuclei are inherently unstable and therefore fissionable. This is a critical concept to understand in reference to the unbelievable power of the nuclear bomb.

An important concept is one of an *isotope*. Let's take the hydrogen atom as the first example. It has been determined that the hydrogen atom not only consists of one electron revolving around one proton, but there are also two other hydrogen atoms. One is deuterium that has one electron revolving around a nucleus consisting of one proton and one neutron. The second isotope of hydrogen has one electron revolving around a nucleus consisting of one proton and two neutrons. This isotope of hydrogen is tritium. There's very little deuterium and tritium, but they are there. The atoms are all electrically neutral but have different weights because of the extra neutrons. Other elements have isotopes as well, but we will jump to uranium because of its relevance to our story. Uranium is U-238 because of the number of protons and neutrons in the nucleus. But there is also U-235, U-233, and U-234. By definition then, the U-235 has three less neutrons than U-238. U-235 is critically important as this is the isotope of uranium that is most radioactive and relevant to our story.

As atoms break down it becomes clear that the original atom will become less and less over time. How much of the original substance will be left over a given period? The way this is calculated is by the concept of half-life. In other words if it takes one year for half of the original atoms to break down leaving half of the original material, then in the next year half of the half that remained will break down. This will leave one-quarter of the original material, which will break down in the next year leaving one-eighth of the original material, and so ad infinitum.

Uranium is a naturally occurring *radioactive* element. A radioactive element undergoes a natural and spontaneous process—the emission of excess energy in the form of particles or waves (it breaks down). These

173

energy emissions or *ionizing radiations*, are extremely high in energy and are easily detected and measured. The high energy of the radioactive material affects anything with which it comes in contact. The energy removes electrons from the atoms of whatever they strike, and that includes the human body. The effects can be fatal. It is known as radiation sickness or poisoning.

When the atom of the radioactive element emits this energy, it may give rise either to a lower energy form of the same atom, or a different nucleus and therefore a different atom.

Uranium is a naturally occurring radioactive element found in soil, water, rocks, plants and animals, including humans. It is a weakly radioactive substance, but it has powerful effects.

In 1789, Martin Klaproth, a German chemist, isolated uranium from the mineral pitchblende. In 1896, Henri Becquerel, a French physicist, working with pure uranium, was the first to discover the process of radioactivity.

Naturally occurring uranium has an *atomic mass* of 238. This number refers to the amount of particles within the nucleus of the atom. In this case, the uranium atomic nucleus contains 146 *neutrons* (neutral particles) and ninety-two *protons* (positively charged particles). To balance the positive charge within the nucleus there are ninety-two electrons (negatively charged) revolving around the nucleus in many-shelled circles, or orbits.

The *half-life* of uranium—that is, the time for one-half of the uranium to undergo *radioactive decay*—is 4.47 billion years. Because of this long half-life, the amount of uranium on the earth during our lifetime stays about the same.

As mentioned above, naturally occurring uranium has three different isotopes. An isotope is a form of an element with a different atomic mass. For uranium, the isotopes are U-238, U-235 and U-234. All of the uranium isotopes are radioactive. The half-life of U-235 is 400 million years. The half-life of U-234 is 246,000 years. U-238 constitutes 99.27 percent of all uranium. U-235 is 0.72 percent and U-234 is 0.0055 percent.

Uranium isotopes are separated from each other in a process called *enrichment*. The purpose of the enrichment process is to accumulate the *enriched fraction (U-235)*, used in nuclear reactors and in the manufacture of nuclear bombs. The uranium remaining after the enrichment process is virtually all U-238, known as *depleted uranium* and this is a very hard metal that has some military uses.

There are multiple steps involved in the process of taking uranium ore and turning it into fissionable material for a nuclear bomb. The uranium ore, mined from the earth, is combined with sulfuric acid, which leaches out pure uranium. Next, the uranium is dried and turned into a coarse powder (*yellowcake*) by a filtering process. The yellowcake, exposed to flourine gas and heated to 133 degrees Fahrenheit converts the uranium into a gas called uranium hexaflouride. The gaseous uranium, spun in a series of centrifuges separates the heavier U-238 from the lighter U-235. Enriched uranium is a twenty percent concentration of U-235. After about a year of repeated centrifuging, the concentration of U-235 will be ninety percent. This process results in highly enriched uranium used to make nuclear bombs, but first it requires conversion into a metal powder, uranium oxide. The uranium oxide, molded into a sphere weighing between thirty-five to 100 pounds is the actual weapon.

The reason U-235 is appropriate for nuclear reactors or nuclear bombs is that U-235 can *fission* or split. This means that if a moving free neutron strikes the nucleus of U-235 it has the power to cause the nucleus to fission, or split into smaller fragments. If some of the smaller fragments are other neutrons, they can hit other atoms and cause them to split also. On the average, when one neutron hits the nucleus of U-235 it liberates two neutrons that, in turn, hit two more nuclei liberating four neutrons, hitting four more nuclei liberating eight neutrons etcetera for about eighty doublings—all continuing in a millionth of a second causing a *sustained nuclear chain reaction*. The process works better when the neutron slows down allowing it to stay in the uranium atomic nucleus longer and thus amplifying the fission process. Using a substance called a *moderator* (graphite or heavy water) slows neutrons down.

The fission process, if controlled, creates energy that converts into electricity to power our cities. If uncontrolled, a nuclear explosion will result.

THE END

AUTHOR BIOGRAPHY

A graduate of the University of Illinois College of Medicine, Sheldon Cohen has practiced internal medicine, served as a medical director of the Alexian Brother's Medical Center in Northwest Suburban Chicago (now Amita), and served as the medical director of two managed care organizations: Cigna Health plan of Illinois and Humanicare Plus of Illinois. The author taught internal medicine and physical diagnosis to medical students from Loyola University Stritch School of Medicine and the Chicago Medical School. Recognizing the fact that busy physicians are pressed for time and thus often fail to capture a thorough medical history, the author perfected one of the first computerized medical history systems for private practice and wrote a paper on his experience with 1500 patients who utilized the system. This was one of the early efforts in promoting electronic health records, a work in progress to this day. Serving as a consultant for Joint Commission Resources of the Joint Commission on Accreditation of Healthcare Organizations, the author did quality consultations at hospitals in the United States, Rio de Janeiro, Brazil, Copenhagen, Denmark, and served as a consultant to the Ministry of Health in Ukraine, assisting them in the development of a hospital accrediting body.

Dr. Cohen is the author of 35 books.

Printed in the United States
By Bookmasters